KNIGHT OF MAYHEM

THE KNIGHTS OF THE ANARCHY
(BOOK 4)

SHERRY EWING

© Copyright 2024 by Sherry Ewing
Text by Sherry Ewing
Cover by Kim Killion Designs

Dragonblade Publishing, Inc. is an imprint of Kathryn Le Veque Novels, Inc.
P.O. Box 23
Moreno Valley, CA 92556
ceo@dragonbladepublishing.com

Produced in the United States of America

First Edition November 2024
Print Edition

Reproduction of any kind except where it pertains to short quotes in relation to advertising or promotion is strictly prohibited.

All Rights Reserved.

The characters and events portrayed in this book are fictitious. Any similarity to real persons, living or dead, is purely coincidental and not intended by the author.

ARE YOU SIGNED UP FOR DRAGONBLADE'S BLOG?

You'll get the latest news and information on exclusive giveaways, exclusive excerpts, coming releases, sales, free books, cover reveals and more.

Check out our complete list of authors, too!

No spam, no junk. That's a promise!

Sign Up Here

www.dragonbladepublishing.com

Dearest Reader;

Thank you for your support of a small press. At Dragonblade Publishing, we strive to bring you the highest quality Historical Romance from some of the best authors in the business. Without your support, there is no 'us', so we sincerely hope you adore these stories and find some new favorite authors along the way.

Happy Reading!

CEO, Dragonblade Publishing

Additional Dragonblade books by Author Sherry Ewing

The Knights of the Anarchy Series
Knight of Darkness (Book 1)
Knight of Chaos (Book 2)
Knight of Havoc (Book 3)
Knight of Mayhem (Book 4)

The Lyon's Den Series
To Claim a Lyon's Heart
The Lyon and His Promise
Only a Lyon Will Do

Knight of Mayhem:
The Knights of the Anarchy (Book Four)
By Sherry Ewing

Torn between duty and love, can a knight and a woman warrior forget they are enemies and let love into their hearts?

As one of Empress Matilda's most trusted knights, Lord Richard Grancourt helps plan his monarch's escape when Oxford Castle is held under siege by King Stephen's army. When a woman in Stephen's forces discovers their plan, Richard is tasked with remaining behind and keeping her silent.

Lady Annora de Maris will do anything to save her son, who has been King Stephen's hostage since his men killed her husband and took her home. Though she's forced to raise her sword against King Stephen's enemies, her loyalties are secretly with the Empress she's compelled to fight against.

Richard takes Annora captive, but his tactics challenge his beliefs about honor and justice, and his feelings for Annora conflict with his duty.

As the mayhem of war pulls Richard and Annora apart, can love overcome the barriers that separate them?

Dedication

For my friend Bill.

Without your words of encouragement all those years ago, I don't know that I would have taken those first steps to become a published author. Thank you for helping me see that it was still possible to achieve my dreams. This one is for you…

PROLOGUE

In the time known today as the Anarchy, England was torn between two enemies, each claiming a right to the throne. Some of England's nobles pledged their allegiance to Stephen and declared him king whilst others cast their fate with Empress Matilda, the daughter of Henry I. This unrest placed most of the country into a state of civil war lasting for almost a score of years. Many knights bore the burden of fighting for either side, each determined to win the land for whomever they served.

Amongst such knights were three brothers and another knight who was the brother of their heart. These four swore to defend the Empress Matilda and her rightful claim to England's crown. The Norwood brothers were close in age. Wymar was the eldest and jumped at the chance to swear his oath of fealty to the Empress after their parents were killed in Stephen's raid on Brockenhurst Castle. Ousted from the only home he had known six years ago, Wymar plunged himself and his brothers into war all in the hopes that when the Empress was crowned queen, she would reward his loyalty with the return of his lands and his title.

Theobald was next and the peacekeeper amongst them. He was used to following his eldest brother, no matter that he would prefer to sit in front of a fire to rest his weary feet with a mug of ale in his hand. Reynard, the youngest, was always attempting to prove his worth even when the odds were stacked against him. He was more like his eldest brother than he would ever admit, even to himself. And

Richard, the brother of their heart, fought beside them all.

The four of them swore to remain together as a family as they had no one else on whom they could rely. But things changed as the war progressed. The first change was when Brockenhurst and Wymar's title were restored. Wymar had wed, as had Theobald, both of them settled happily in loving marriages, holding estates in the Empress's name. Reynard, too, had married, but he and his wife, Elysande, still served their Empress. This left Richard to continue to follow the Empress until he, too, was released from his service. His sister Beatrix was also residing at court, and he cursed the day he had been tasked with her care. If he did not find her a husband soon, he feared she would come to ruin.

There is a beginning, a middle, and an end for each tale of the knights of the Anarchy. This is Richard's story...

CHAPTER ONE

Oxford, England
December 1142

Lord Richard Grancourt paced his sister's bedchamber like a caged animal, pondering all that had brought him to this moment.

He had followed the Norwood brothers into the war that had raged throughout England for a decade. That his own estate neighboring Brockenhurst had not suffered at King Stephen's hands had been a miracle. He was grateful to have a home to return to, and to know that his parents continued to live there peacefully, but his chosen place had been on the battlefront, fighting for the cause he believed in. His loyalty to the Empress was absolute…even when she gave him the most annoying of tasks, such as fetching his spoiled younger sister so she might join the Empress as one of her ladies-in-waiting.

Beatrix had a frivolous nature—unsurprising, after the way their parents always doted upon the girl. She had come to expect that she would always be allowed to have whatever she wanted and to do whatever she pleased, which might explain how she had scared off all of her suitors. That she was now an unwed woman of a score and four years did not sit well with Richard. He felt that 'twas up to him to find her a suitable husband, but he was under no illusions that 'twould be a simple task.

Up until recently, that need to see his sister properly settled had been the greatest task weighing on his mind…but then the castle had been put under siege. The walls protected them from harm, but supplies were running low, and there was no rescue coming. A desperate plan had been formed to allow the Empress to escape, aided by some of her most trusted men—including Richard. 'Twas all scheduled to take place on the morrow, and he was still uncertain how much he should share with Beatrix. 'Twas far from certain that she could be trusted to keep silent. But could he leave without telling her goodbye? If things went poorly, he might not see her again this side of heaven.

"Do sit down, Richard, before you give me a headache with all your pacing," Beatrix warned. "Is it not enough that I am all but starving here?"

Richard turned his blue eyes to his sister. Her hair was as black as his own but that was the end to their resemblance. Her eyes were brown, and her body was petite in frame. She was a rare beauty, for all that she had a troublesome temperament.

Richard finally shook his thoughts from his head and did as Beatrix bid. He took a chair next to her as she continued to hold one hand up to her forehead. Her cheeks were gaunt, the sight filling him with remorse that he had not been able to provide for her. As much as he disagreed with his sibling on almost everything, he did not like to see her suffer.

He reached for her free hand. "I know 'tis difficult, Beatrix. But recall, you are not the only one hungry, Beatrix. We are all in the same position with empty bellies each eve."

"I want to go home," she complained bitterly turning pleading eyes to him.

He gave a heavy sigh. "Aye, as do we all. But there is nothing to be done but to continue to serve Empress Matilda."

Beatrix leaned back in her chair before she narrowed her eyes. "What are you not telling me, Richard? You must have some news. 'Tis not like you to keep secrets between us."

A harumph left him. The men might call him the Knight of Mayhem, speaking in awed whispers of his prowess on the battlefield, the way his strikes could never be predicted, always catching the enemy by surprise. But when it came to his sister, it seemed he could hide nothing. She had always been able to read him like a book. Telling Beatrix of the plans for the morrow could put the Empress and the entire escape plan in jeopardy, but how could he keep it from her? She was right to say that he did not like secrets between them.

"Beatrix... you must needs know that if there was another way..."

She gave an exasperated shout of displeasure. "Out with it, Richard. There is no sense keeping me in the dark about whatever is about to transpire!" she demanded. "My nerves have already reached the breaking point. I am beyond exhausted from this blasted siege lasting for months with no end in sight."

Richard ran his fingers through his hair. He understood his sister's frustration with being confined. There was not much to look forward to and a Christmas celebration in a couple of weeks was certainly not about to happen. There was not much to celebrate.

"Very well," he began but then pointed a warning finger at her. "But I tell you this in the strictest of confidence."

She raised one of her dark brows. "Then tell me and stop putting things off."

"On the morrow, the Empress has plans to make her escape in the middle of the night," Richard stated before Beatrix interrupted him by jumping up from her chair.

"What? How does she think we shall travel in the dead of night? Or did she forget 'tis the middle of winter?" she fumed. She stomped over to where a pitcher had been set. She picked up the container to peer inside only to slam it back down. Clearly, the wine it had once held was now gone.

He took a deep breath before he returned to his explanation. "You shall be staying here along with the Empress's other attendants. This must needs be a small party to sneak past Stephen's army."

Beatrix had gone around the table and now leaned her hands upon the edges. "Are you trying to inform me that you are leaving me here? And that you shall be gone for who knows how long?"

"Aye."

Another sound of outrage came from her lips and she swept her hand over the contents of the table, sending objects flying. Richard ducked as a chalice came soaring toward his head.

"You cannot leave me!" she cried out.

He quickly stood and went to take his sister in his arms, but she pushed him away. "Enough, Beatrix. You must remain strong."

"Strong? You must be jesting with me, you dolt. How can I be strong when I am all but wasting away here without nourishment?"

"Once the usurper Stephen realizes that the Empress is no longer inside Oxford, he will have no choice but to allow those left behind to surrender," Richard reasoned as she began to cry. "Please, little sister… if I could take you with me I would, but you would not fare well out there trekking through the snow for miles. You are safer right here."

She stomped her foot in protest before raising her eyes to meet his. "How can you leave me here to starve?"

"You will not go hungry for much longer. I promise," he whispered before attempting once more to pull her into his arms. This time, she allowed it.

"You should not make promises, Richard, that you may not be able to keep," she whined hiding her face against his chest.

He took her chin to tip her head so she could view him again. "You will not go hungry for much longer," he repeated. "Promise me you will keep this conversation between just us."

She gave a huff of despair. "I may be spoiled but I am not a fool, Richard. You have my word."

He kissed her forehead. "I will see you soon."

"If you say so," she pouted.

He began making his way toward the door to return to the Empress's solar. "Try not to miss me too much, sister," he teased, giving her a wink.

Her lips twitched as she tried to suppress the smile that nearly overtook her pout. He opened the door but stopped when she called his name. "Richard… be safe," she murmured quietly.

"I will," he promised, and then closed the door. He made his way back down the passageway to the Empress's solar where those who were in her confidence continued to plot out their plan. Richard could only ponder in amazement if such a ruse would actually work. They would find out on the morrow.

CHAPTER TWO

Lady Annora de Maris strode across the frozen winter ground to the sound of crunching snow beneath her feet. 'Twas bitterly cold and she could see her breath on each exhale. Sir Merek Baringar, the knight who had once been captain of her guard, strode next to her. She had been thankful when he'd agreed to follow her when she was unwillingly torn from Meregate Castle. Her reputation as a fierce warrior had been her downfall after her husband had been killed during a siege of their home. King Stephen's men had informed him of her skill as a fighter, and he had demanded that she place those skills under his banner, using her son as leverage against her. Just thinking of it made her want to scream.

But what good would shrieking do? Nothing! They would not return her husband to her, nor would they earn the release of her son, Leif, from the cruel man who pretended to be England's rightful king. But if she had to force herself to serve him to earn her son's release, then so be it.

"You will not gain much if you continue to scowl, Annora," Merek warned whilst blowing warm air into his hands. Even the leather of their gloves could not prevent the cold from seeping into their bones.

"I do not wish to gain anything from *that* man except my freedom and that of my son."

A rumble of discontent came from Merek. "I highly doubt you could be that lucky."

"What do you suppose he wants from me this time?" she asked

gazing up to her most faithful knight. Though she viewed him as a brother, she could see that he was a handsome man with tawny-colored hair much like her own and blue eyes. Merek should be off getting married and raising his children instead of following her into this mess. But she honored the loyalty that kept him by her side, and she trusted his council.

"Most likely to gloat over the fact he controls you. What other reason might a king wish to see you?"

She raised her brow at the implication of his words. "Nothing of *that* nature, I assure you. If Stephen is nothing else, he remains faithful to his wife, Queen Matilda."

A grunt left him as they continued forward toward Stephen's tent. "Then the only advice I can offer you for whatever may happen is to keep calm and control your emotions. 'Twill not do you or your son any good if your temper gets the better of you."

A sob caught in her throat at the thought of her son, left to the care of others at only seven summers. She swiped at a tear that leaked from the corner of her eye. She supposed if she were home and her husband yet lived, her son might be getting ready to be fostered by one of her husband's allies. Now, she could only worry over his fate.

She squared back her shoulders as they neared Stephen's tent. "I will remain... civil," she said through pursed lips.

A short laugh escaped Merek. "I will enjoy watching you try."

She turned her gaze toward him. "Why do I put up with you?" she said attempting to keep the humor from her tone.

"Because I remain you most trusted servant, my lady."

"You are my *only* servant, Baringar, if I can even call you that these days."

"Whatever you shall call me, I still serve the de Maris household. Until you release me from the vow I took, then I shall remain at your side," Merek declared when they reached the tent. He gave her a short bow and she nodded her head. He had more than proved his worth on too many occasions to count. She would not doubt his words now.

She waited for the knight who stood at the opening to the tent to fold back the flap to allow her entrance. When he continued to stand there inspecting her, unmoving, she finally voiced her complaint. "King Stephen is expecting me."

The man pointed toward Merek. "Aye. His Majesty is expecting *you*, Lady de Maris. *He* can wait here."

Merek stepped forward, no doubt intending to challenge this order, but Annora placed her hand upon his forearm. "I will be fine. Wait here," she said. He frowned but gave a short nod of understanding and stepped back. The knight at last opened the flap of the tent so Annora could enter.

This was not the first time Annora had been summoned to appear before King Stephen, but the opulence of the king's living quarters whilst on campaign still sent her head reeling. To say he traveled in luxury was an understatement. 'Twas though he wished to convey his wealth to anyone who had the dubious privilege to be in his presence.

A banner proclaiming his house was a backdrop to the golden chair that acted as his throne. Silken linens hung from the roof to cascade around the room in a colorful display. If Annora did not know better, she would have thought she had entered a sultan's tent instead of that of England's king. Golden cups and platters holding all manner of food sat on a table. A bed covered with fur blankets would keep the cold from any man even without the roaring fire that was lit in the center. Grey smoke lifted to the top of the tent where an opening allowed the plumes to escape. All in all, King Stephen lived in the lap of absurdly opulent luxury whilst his people starved in the outside world.

The man himself finally lifted his gaze from a map he was perusing with several of his lieutenants. "That will be all," King Stephen said whilst the men bowed and began to depart. He had, at least, the look of a king. Stephen was a well-built man with wavy brown hair and eyes. His hair fell to his shoulders and a beard covered his face. A fur mantel adorned his shoulders and Annora could see a purple-colored tunic beneath his cloak when he turned to go and take a seat at his throne.

"Lady de Maris... prompt as always," the King began as he waved his hand toward her. "Do come forward and pay homage to your king."

Merek's words repeated themselves inside her head and she added her own mantra of *keep calm, keep calm, keep calm* to go with them. The King held out his hand for her and when she stood before him, she dropped down onto one knee, took his hand, and kissed the signet ring on one of his fingers. She let the monarch's hand go as quickly as she had taken it and waited for permission to rise. Her head bowed, she continued to wait in silence until an amused chuckle finally left his lips.

"You do so keep me entertained, Lady de Maris... even if 'tis just briefly," the King exclaimed. "You may rise."

Gaining her feet, she placed her feet slightly apart and clasped her hands behind her as any other knight would have done. She focused her gaze not on the man but a point behind him on the colored tapestry portraying his house and self-appointed station in life. A grim reminder that to Annora, this man was the usurper and not the rightful ruler of England.

"Look at me!" he ordered sharply forcing Annora to turn her green eyes to the man who held her son in captivity. "Even in my own tent you dare to defy me."

"You asked for an audience with me, and I am here, Your Majesty," Annora replied in a calm, even tone. "What can I do to appease your anger with me?"

"You can start by wiping the look of your own anger from your visage. Do you think me a fool?" the King asked in his own tense tone.

"Of course not, my liege. I am but your most humble servant," she answered lowering her eyes so she need not look upon this man who was her enemy.

A snort of disbelief fell from his lips. "Humble? You? I would hardly describe you as humble, Lady Annora. I do not believe you even know the meaning of the word."

"I serve you as faithfully as any of your other knights. How else am I to earn my son's freedom?" She clenched her hands together behind her back as she once again leveled her eyes upon the king.

"Your son will be granted his freedom when your service to me is at an end and not before," King Stephen said whilst a corner of his mouth lifted in a smirk.

"And how soon might that be, Your Highness?" she inquired.

King Stephen shrugged. "With Empress Matilda captured inside Oxford Castle and starving to death, I suppose this siege may not go on much longer."

A spark of hope filled her heart that mayhap she would soon be allowed to go home. "Perchance you would allow me—"

"But this does not mean you will be allowed to go free. I am certain you can still prove valuable to me. After all, your ability with a sword is just as good as any of my other protectors."

And then he dashed that spark of hope away as quickly as he had lit it. She narrowed her eyes and clenched her jaw so she did not allow the bitter words to fall from her lips. As Merek told her, no good would come if she did not remain civil to the man who held her and her son's lives in his hands.

"If that is all then, Your Majesty, may I return to my tent?" she asked hoping he would allow her to leave his stifling presence before her hold on her temper finally snapped.

He stood and came directly before her. Reaching out, he took her chin between his long fingers to tilt her head so she had no choice but to stare directly at her enemy.

"You may hate me, Annora, but you shall continue to serve me as your king for as long as I deem necessary. Your service to my cause *will* be accomplished to the best of your ability, or you will not like the consequences. Keep your opinions to yourself and do not let me hear again of your complaints you have vocalized in camp. Morale is low enough during these winter months and I do not need you adding to the men's emotional discontent. Do I make myself clear?"

"Aye, Your Majesty," she slowly murmured, ruing that she had let her feelings get the better of her the other night when she and Merek had been in the tent to grab their evening meal. Apparently, word of it had traveled back to the King.

"Then I give you permission to leave until the next time you are summoned, Lady de Maris," he replied letting go of her chin. Another smirk swept across his mouth before he returned to the table where he once again looked over the map laid out before him. She was dismissed.

She left the tent with Merek following behind her. Their silence continued until they could return to her tent, where they would have the privacy they needed to have a conversation between them. But would it be private enough? She was being watched more closely than she had realized. The thought made her cringe in worry. She could only ponder who amongst them had the king's ear to inform him of her every move.

CHAPTER THREE

RICHARD STOOD IN the Empress's bedchamber with the other knights who would join them this eve. Reynard and Elysande Norwood stood whispering to one another in a corner of the room. Newly married, they were lucky in that they would not be torn from one another's side. The others were Blake Kennarde and Kingsley Goodee whom he had fought beside since the Battle of Lincoln over a year ago. Their other comrade in arms, Oswin Woodwarde had been none too pleased to be told he would remain behind to guard the Empress's ladies in waiting.

Richard looked over the map of Oxford Castle and the outlying area one last time wondering how their party would make it past Stephen's army that had them surrounded. But staying was not an option. Supplies were running out, and the harbor was also blocked from what they could gather, keeping their allies from coming to liberate them. Their initial hope that the Empress's half-brother Robert of Gloucester would arrive at any time had diminished whilst each day had rolled into the next.

'Twas now almost mid-December and they had been held inside these walls since September. And while the Empress had sent her calvary out to seek those who still favored her before the gates closed months ago, no one had been able to come to her aid or bring reinforcements. She was tired, cold, and hungry as were the rest of them, and she had determined that she would no longer stay idly by and starve to death. Instead, she had planned her own escape.

"You are certain, my Empress, that you wish to proceed," Richard asked one last time. As much as he understood her reasons for wishing to escape, the risks were so great that he still held on to hope that she might change her mind.

"Aye, Grancourt. I will not let Stephen determine my fate nor will he keep me under his thumb another day longer."

"Then let us away and pray to God that all will be in our favor," Richard said before heading to the door. Their small party followed him.

They quietly made their way down the passageway, down one of the back stairs, and through the deserted kitchen. At this hour of the night, all was quiet. The fresh fallen snow that blanketed the earth would fit in perfectly with the empress's plans to make her escape, since the Empress had had her ladies prepare cloaks made of white to help them blend in with the winter wonderland all around them. In this dangerous enterprise, these small precautions could make the difference between safe concealment and a disastrous capture.

They left the keep through the rear door and a blast of frigid cold air almost sucked the breath right out of Richard. But he continued onward toward the postern gate. There could be no denying the brisk chill in the air would hinder their progress. Richard could only hope that Reynard's wife, along with the Empress, would be able to endure what was ahead of them.

Richard turned to quietly address the group before opening the gate door. "Remember... your silence is imperative for this plan to work. We must needs tread carefully once outside this gate as our enemy will be near at every turn."

The Empress took hold of Richard's arm. "Let us proceed, Grancourt. We have a long journey ahead of us once we cross the river."

A brief thought flashed through Richard's mind of the ice cracking on the mighty Thames River that they needed to cross. Drowning in the churning frozen water would be a miserable way to die if the ice did not hold until they reached the other side's bank.

But they would have to risk it. Any chance to change their minds was gone once Richard led them through the postern gate and they all began tip toeing through the forces that were surrounding them. Richard held his breath whilst they made progress over the snow-covered ground. He took a glance over his shoulder and could see that the Empress's cloak was already wet at the hem. Soon the weight of the garment would hinder her ability to move quickly. But their monarch was a woman of iron will and thus far, she showed no signs of lagging. Their luck held and no one confronted them as they made progress over the frozen ground. Reynard and Elysande exchanged a smile causing Richard to frown. 'Twas too soon to celebrate that they had made their escape.

They were just rounding a tent on the outskirts of the enemy's camp when disaster struck. A knight stepped from his tent bumping straight into Richard.

"You!" a voice hissed.

Before their enemy could sound any sort of an alarm in the still quiet of the night, Richard took hold of the knight and muffled the cry by placing his hand over the captive's mouth.

The Empress stepped forward. "You know this person, Grancourt?" she softly asked before looking in every direction for another guard to jump out at them.

"Aye, my Empress, and *he* is a *she*," Richard answered taking a firm hold of the woman he had previously encountered not only at Winchester but also fought against at this very castle in September.

Reynard pulled Elysande closer whilst they tried to reassess their dire situation with this new complication. "Bloody hell," he murmured.

The Empress looked at the young woman who glared at those around her with hatred flashing in her eyes. "This changes our plans only somewhat. Take her back to the castle, Grancourt, since you are previously acquainted with this… *lady*. Norwood, you take the lead whilst Elysande stays with me. Kennarde and Goodee can bring up the rear and watch for threats from behind."

Richard pulled the struggling woman closer before turning to Reynard. "Be as quiet as possible as sound will travel. Watch them all and above all your back."

"Aye, I will, and you do the same, brother," Reynard replied before kissing his wife's cheek and turning to leave.

Richard wished he could say more in the way of a farewell to the man. Reynard was like a younger brother to him, much like Wymar and Theobald. But there was no time for sentiments. Not when the woman he held began to squirm in his arms.

"Let us away and be quiet," he ordered as he began pulling the woman back toward the castle. But she was not an easy conquest to bend to his will. Though he was larger and stronger, she refused to submit and she did her best to free herself from his grasp.

She kicked, pulled, and pushed him until Richard felt his shins would never recover. When she drew her knee up, she narrowly missed his privates and Richard growled in frustration. This was certainly not what he had expected would go wrong with their night. There was, however, a certain amount of satisfaction knowing he had finally caught this troublesome woman who had escaped him for nigh unto a year!

They finally neared the postern gate and Richard called up to get the attention of one of the guards above. A few minutes later, the gate was opened and Richard, along with his captive, slipped through the door before it once more slammed shut.

He was about to let go of her mouth when she bit his gloved hand. He let out a cry, more of shock than of pain, and released the woman, allowing her to go free. She began to run away from him—but where she thought she was going Richard had no idea. He easily caught up with her and took hold of her arm once more.

"You little hellcat," he cursed tearing off his glove and feeling the slight imprint of her teeth marking his flesh.

"You have no right to take me captive," she sneered in contempt. "Let me go and no other harm will befall you."

Damn but she is a bold one, he thought whilst he lifted one dark brow. "You are not going anywhere. You slipped away from me at Winchester and months ago before this castle fell, but you shall not get away so easily this time."

"Winchester? I do not recall fighting you there," she said frowning.

"There was a lot going on. Mayhap you did not notice me—but I noticed *you*," Richard began. "You were fighting with another woman knight… red hair… I am certain you must remember *her*."

The lady's eyes widened as though his words had stirred her memory. "She would be hard to forget. There are not many women who would dare fight for a cause they believe in."

"And you believe in Stephen's cause?" Richard asked guiding her through the bailey.

She shrugged. "His cause has as much merit as does the Empress's, I suppose."

A snort left Richard. "If you believe he is the rightful ruler, then 'tis a good thing you will no longer fight on his behalf."

"You know nothing about me or my reasons for doing what I must. You have no right—"

"I have every right," he bellowed before checking his anger. "You killed enough of my comrades between the last two battles. You shall not go free to continue fighting in Stephen's name."

"Where are you taking me?" she questioned him, making an attempt to dig her boots into the snow beneath their feet. Such an effort did not have the desired results and only caused her to stumble into him when he gave a hard yank on her arm.

They came chest to chest and Richard could imagine how every inch of her glorious body would feel against his if he had not been wearing his chainmail. She had evidently been on her way to take care of her personal business, for she only wore tunic and hose beneath her cloak. Her chest heaved whilst taking in large gulps of air.

The moon decided to peek out from behind the clouds and Richard was at last able to take a leisurely look upon the lady. Tawny hair that reminded him of a lion's fur framed a round face with a pert nose. Full red lips were parted slightly before she bit her lower lip as she raised green eyes up to him. If he did not consider her his enemy, he would have been tempted to bend forward and seal those lips with a kiss. She was a tempting vixen, but he would not fall for her ploy to gain his confidence and trust.

Nay! He would not allow this lady to cloud his thoughts. Instead of giving in to his baser instincts, he pulled her toward the kitchen entrance to the keep. Once inside, he continued onward until he came before the turrets that held his own bedchamber. He continued dragging her along up the winding stairs. When they reached his room, he opened the door and pushed her inside before slamming the bolt into place.

"You shall sleep in here with me until I know I can trust you," Richard began before he held up his hand to halt her protest, "and that is not open to negotiation. Be happy you are not residing in the Empress's pit."

He went across the room to use some of the last remaining firewood to warm the room. Once the fire was going, he motioned for her to take a chair. Turning away from the woman who threw him a warning glare, he removed his cloak and flung it over the wooden chest at the foot of his bed. He stared at the mattress wondering what in the bloody hell he was going to do with her now!

CHAPTER FOUR

ANNORA FOLDED HER arms over her chest after declining his silent request to sit. Instead, she took a moment to study the man who held her against her will. When he had taken off his white cloak, strands of his short-cropped black hair stood on end. He threw the garment on the chest at the foot of his bed and her breath caught in her throat. God's bones! Surely, he would not take her against her will, would he? She hoped he had more honor than that, but the truth was that she knew nothing about this knight other than what she had seen with her own eyes on the battlefield.

She had lied when she pretended not to recall seeing him during the battle at Winchester. Of course she had noted such a magnificent fighter. There was no doubt he was an accomplished swordman for she had witnessed his skill with a blade both at Winchester and at this very castle. But her encounter with another woman who fought for her own cause had given Annora pause to acknowledge the lady's skill. When she saw this very man coming toward her on the battlefield, Annora had fled to avoid a confrontation with him.

'Twas not the first time such a weakness had overcome her. She had been about at her breaking point back in September when their blades had met that fateful day outside of the city of Oxford's gates. If others fighting for Stephen had not come to her aid, she might have suffered a devasting blow. She had been lucky but obviously such luck had run its course given her present predicament.

"What is your name?" the knight quietly asked running his hand through his hair.

"Does my name honestly matter to you?" she returned tartly.

He swirled around so quickly that Annora jumped back. Even though he remained several steps away, she could not help but feel inadequately small compared to a man who must be at least six feet tall.

He took several menacing steps in her direction, and she lifted her chin hoping to give him the impression she was unafraid of him. "I asked you a question," he said through clenched teeth.

"Aye, you did." She began tapping her boot upon the floor. She finally looked him in the eye and she tried to hold back her surprise. Blue... his eyes were an incredible shade of blue. Their color was one she would most likely not soon forget. Blue eyes and black hair... the combination had always been her downfall, but she swore she would not allow this man to get the better of her.

"Will you make me wait the remainder of the night to learn what you are called?"

"Perchance... will I end up waiting as many hours to learn what you plan to do with me?"

He pulled her forward once again and she had no other choice but to place her palms on his chest to keep herself from pressing against him with her entire body. "I can tell you are going to be a handful and not allow me a moment's peace."

"What did you expect when you captured a woman in the middle of the night to hold her against her will?"

An unexpected chuckle left him before he let her go and proceeded to take a blanket from the foot of the bed. With his back to her, Annora was finally able to breathe. "You have certainly lived up to my recollections of you, my lady."

She watched his back wondering what he would do or say next. He certainly did not seem bent on having his wicked way with her. He put the blanket back down before turning toward her again and striding over to stand before her.

"I am Lord Richard Grancourt," he said by way of introduction. He then gave her a slight bow. He stood there waiting for her reply. After a few moments of silence, it became clear that their conversation would not continue until she answered him.

"Lady Annora de Maris," she said, refraining from giving any other information about where she hailed.

"De Maris?" he asked, and she only nodded. "The name sounds familiar to me."

Annora shrugged. "'Tis a common enough name, I suppose."

"'Twill come to me eventually but for now at least we know what to call one another," Richard declared, stepping forward. He began inspecting her. Annora stepped away from him, her worries renewed that mayhap he was indeed bent on taking her.

A smirk spread across his face as he quickly reached out and unfastened the belt around her waist that held her scabbard. It dropped to the floor, but he was not done inspecting her for hidden weapons. She screeched in outrage as he began patting down her body. She did her best to fight him off. Her elbow met his stomach, her boot kicked at his shin—but he was undeterred. He found the knife tucked away behind her back in the waist of her hose and that, too, fell to the floor. He pulled her over to a chair and the next thing she knew she was forced onto his lap.

"Let me go!" she said, squirming as she demanded to be released.

"As soon as I know you no longer have anything to plunge into me whilst we sleep."

"'Tis the first thing I will do when I am able," she retorted, remaining defiant even as she was firmly held in his grasp.

"Hence my inspection of your person," Richard retorted. Despite her protests, she knew his precautions were well founded. She supposed she would have done the same if their situation had been reversed.

Annora pushed on his chest to put some sort of distance between them, but to no avail. If anything, she swore his arms only tightened around her, bringing them chest to chest. She began to realize that any further moment on her part might just cause a part of him to become aroused. That would certainly not help her cause to remain untouched.

"I do not have any further weapons on me," she said, lying.

"And I am certain you are spewing a falsehood."

She could not hold back her cry of surprise when she was suddenly flipped over onto her stomach. Her head now almost touched the floor with her bottom upward in a most undignified manner. "I am so tempted," he said before he reached for her boots and gave them a tug. The sound of one dirk and then a second as the other boot was removed now told Annora she was completely at this man's mercy. He pulled her up again and she had no choice but to stare into his eyes when he brought her close.

"I hate you," she jeered pushing again on his chest to no avail.

"I am certain you do but we are stuck with each other… at least for now." He pushed back some of her hair that had fallen across her face, and she could sense the calluses along his fingertips and palms. This was no man of leisure. He was a trained warrior, and she could expect nothing from him other than for him to be her enemy.

"You are a fair maiden, Annora, and one who was meant to be kissed often," Richard said whilst continuing to stare upon her.

She was no maiden having been married before… but mayhap if he thought she was still a maid, the lie might work in her favor to be left untouched. "I suppose you think you are man enough to see the matter done properly?"

Another chuckle left him and he took both her cheeks in his rough palms so she was forced to watch him. "Perchance… but not this night. The eve has had many unexpected surprises. One of which was you."

"No one told you to take me captive, Grancourt," she hissed. He quickly stood and Annora stumbled to keep her balance. He held her about her waist until she was steady.

"Nay, you were not a part of our plans, but you are here now and we must needs deal with one another," he replied slowly as he gathered her weapons from the floor and went back over to the chest.

She had not noticed the lock upon it but now he took a key from a pouch at his belt. A loud click sounded as the padlock was opened and her weapons placed inside. The lock was once more put into place, and she watched him put the key away. She doubted she would be able to get the key away from him, but mayhap she would be able to pick the lock whilst he slept. He grabbed the blanket and went to the door. His sword was placed next to the fabric, and he began to lay down right in front of the only route of escape.

"You may take the bed, Annora," Richard finally said as he settled his fully clothed body upon the hard stone floor.

Undressing in front of him was unthinkable so she warily climbed onto the bed to lay on the farthest side away from him. When she heard a soft snore escape from the man who chose the uncomfortable floor instead of his own bed, she was finally able to relax. She fluffed the pillow beneath her head. As she began to finally ease into sleep, she swore the woodsy sent of a perfect stranger soothed her into the best night's sleep she had in years.

CHAPTER FIVE

RICHARD RUSHED WITH Beatrix down the passageway to return to his bedchamber. Several servants carried multiple gowns that Beatrix had hoped would fit the lady he had left with Oswin Woodwarde standing guard outside the door.

"Tell me again why you took her, Richard," Beatrix demanded, her voice filled with disbelief. "'Tis highly unlike you for you to take a woman as your prisoner."

He halted their progress before speaking over Beatrix's shoulder to the servants waiting for his orders. "Proceed. We will follow momentarily." The servants quickly filed past them before Richard gave an exasperated sigh and began pacing back and forth in the passageway. "What else was I to do when she all but ran directly into me from her tent? One scream and she would have alerted the entire camp."

"The Empress would have been captured," Beatrix stated the obvious.

"'Twas impulsive, I know, but the alternative was worse—and 'tis not like I was given any choice on the matter. We could not afford to allow the Empress's plans to all go awry before we even reached the river. The Empress gave the order. I but followed her commands," Richard replied taking his sister's elbow and guiding her down the corridor again.

"But to take a woman captive. Whatever will you do with her?"

'Twas a good question and one he did not necessarily have a longterm answer for. "For now, I had a bath sent up so she could wash.

The gowns are to see she is at least made comfortable."

Beatrix rose one delicate black brow. "You left her alone?" she said aghast that he would be so careless.

"Of course I did not leave her alone. I had Oswin standing guard at the door." He noticed the sweetest smile cross his sister's features, and the words of his friends months ago returned to his mind. "You favor him."

She shook herself out of whatever was flitting through her head. "Who?"

A grunt left him. "Do not play game with me, sister. Oswin… that is who."

She shrugged as if the man meant nothing to her, but Richard knew better. "He has been kind to me," she finally conceded. "Nothing more."

He halted their progress once more. "Do not get your hopes up where Woodwarde is concerned, Beatrix. He is in service to the Empress and who knows where such a life will take him next."

"You do not think he would make a good husband for me? I thought he was your friend."

"He *is* my friend, but I do not relish the thought of my sister squandering her life away living in a camp as Oswin goes from one battle to the next."

"This blasted war cannot go on forever, Richard. One day 'twill come to an end."

"I can only pray you speak the truth, particularly when it comes to this siege. Now, let us go to my bedchamber so I might introduce you to Lady Annora. I have the feeling the two of you will one day become good friends." He leaned over to kiss her cheek and once he stood tall again he noticed her surprise.

She took his arm as they continued forward. "Friends? With a supporter of Stephen? You must be mad," she said. They rounded the corner and saw Oswin standing guard to the door. She gave the knight a bright smile. "Lord Oswin... how fare thee this day?"

Oswin gave Beatrix a low bow. "Lady Beatrix... you are the bright ray of sunshine lightening my day with your presence."

Richard rolled his eyes. "Good heavens... we do not have time to stand here all day whilst the two of you exchange pleasantries."

"Behave, Richard." Beatrix tapped her brother's arm before she turned her eyes back to the man who so obviously cared for her. "You are too kind, good sir. May I also say you look resplendent this day." Oswin took Beatrix's hand and kissed her knuckles all the while continuing to gaze upon her.

"You two can continue your conversation later. She is still inside?" Richard asked giving Oswin a nudge to bring him out of fawning over Beatrix.

"Where else would she be? Other than the servants who just entered to bring in the mountain of dresses for her to choose from, no one else has entered except the maid who was to assist the lady with her bath."

"Thank you for keeping watch," Richard replied, his hand going to the latch of the door to open it wide.

He should have knocked. He should have immediately slammed the portal shut. But he did not...and now there was no way he would ever forget the vision of Annora's body as she stood in the tub whilst the servant dumped a bucket of rinsing water over her head. Everything moved in slow motion as if time, in truth, stood still.

Her body was pure perfection. He stood there gulping at the woman before him. Firm full breasts above a narrow waist and well-toned shapely legs. Her skin glistened from the water but he could see for himself that if he were to run his hands over her flesh, 'twould be smooth to his touch. She was every inch a seasoned warrior but also a woman who was made to be loved and often. At least that was how she appeared inside his head.

And then everything moved as though time was catching up. Her gasp filled the chamber whilst Annora used one hand in an attempt to cover her breasts and the other her most private female part. Beatrix rushed around him to quickly race across the room to hold up a linen to shield Annora's body from his view.

"You imbecile, Richard. Turn around for heaven's sake," Beatrix ordered over her shoulder.

Richard quickly did as he was told. "My apologies… I did not think."

"Nay! You did not," Annora snapped from across the room. "You ordered me a bath. Did you not think I would make full use of it?"

Beatrix answered for him. "Obviously, my brother did not. Try to forgive him if you can, Lady Annora."

Water splashed as the lady removed herself from the tub and still Richard stood staring at his bedchamber door. He nodded to Oswin who quickly closed it. "Again, I apologize Annora. As my sister Beatrix just said, I hope you will forgive my thoughtlessness."

A snort of surprise left the lady… or so he assumed because such a sound could easily have come from his sister. "You have been nothing but thoughtless from the moment we met, Grancourt. I highly doubt you have a chivalrous bone in your body."

"I would have to disagree with you but then you do not know me any better than I know you, Annora," he said still using her first name. Somehow after seeing her naked dropped all pretense with him and he could not imagine calling her anything else.

A sarcastic laugh filled the chamber. "Well, at least on that account, I can agree with you," Annora proclaimed before she continued. "You may turn. I have a robe on now."

Richard once more turned to face the room. The sight of her was just as striking as when he saw Annora rising from the tub. Her tawny-colored hair was dripping wet and she went to sit by the fire whilst the servant began to untangle the tresses that fell down her back.

"Again, my sincere apologies," Richard said with a short bow.

What else could he do but apologize? He had been a fool to enter so casually. The action had been automatic and he certainly had not thought that he would be disturbing the lady at her bath. He had assumed she had long since finished.

Beatrix came to him and began shooing him from his own bedchamber. "Out with you now. Lady Annora and I will finish getting her ready for whatever the cook will be able to provide to break our fast. You can see the lady later down in the great hall."

"But—"

"You will see her *later*," Beatrix repeated as she opened the door and Oswin gave her a wink.

"Bring her directly to me," he ordered his sister.

"As you wish, brother," Beatrix answered right before his own door slammed behind him.

Richard exchanged a look with Oswin. "I need a drink," he declared whilst his friend attempted not to laugh. "Care to join me?"

"'Tis a bit early in the morn to indulge in spirits."

Richard lifted one brow. "That has not stopped us before."

"If we can find anything, why not?" Oswin replied before placing his arm around Richard's shoulder. "I definitely think you are going to need something strong for whatever comes next with your fair lady."

Richard was about to make a retort that Annora was hardly his but found he could not say the words. *His lady...* such a thought could only make him ponder when or where the lady had begun to somehow weave her way into his heart. But considering how she hated him, the thought made him wish he had never crossed her path.

Aye, he definitely needed a drink.

CHAPTER SIX

Annora watched Richard being ushered from the room by his sister. That the pair were related could not be doubted given how similar their features were. The fact that he had barged into his bedchamber and seen her completely in all her naked glory would rattle her wits for months to come. 'Twas almost worth his embarrassment to witness his startled expression that quickly changed to some form of desire whilst his eyes lingered on her body.

She had seen his heated gaze but briefly before he had been ordered to turn around. But the desire she'd witnessed had most certainly been there, for all the good 'twould do either of them. Their destinies had already been determined by a king and empress who continued to wage a war that had plunged England into the brink of starvation. A war that had placed them on opposite sides. Despite Annora's repugnance for Stephen, she could not cross the man—not while he held her son's fate in his hands. Any fanciful thought Annora might have of some kind of future with the man who had taken her captive would have the inevitable outcome of heartbreak. Better to not get involved and continue to hate the man rather than to let love into her heart.

The maid tugged on a tangled knot in her hair and Annora was brought back to the reality of her situation. She must somehow make her escape. If the King learned of her capture, he might think she had willing turned herself over to Empress Matilda's men—and if he believed that, his revenge was sure to be terrible. Her son's life depended upon her staying in Stephen's good graces. Another tug on the mess the maid was trying to undo was enough for Annora. She was used to managing on her own.

She held out her hand and the comb was placed in her palm. "That will be all. I think I can finish on my own. Besides, I have Lady Beatrix here if I require any further help," Annora said as she watched the servant leave. The fewer people in the room, the greater her chance of making an escape.

Beatrix came to perch herself on the edge of the seat opposite Annora and the two women inspected each other for several minutes before Beatrix spoke up. "My brother is a clod," she began whilst smoothing down the fabric of her dress. "I am certain he gave no thought that you would still be attending to your morning rituals and will make a fuller apology once you see him again."

"Your brother and I are hardly on terms that would be considered friendly, Lady Beatrix," Annora said with a heavy sigh. "He took me captive against my will and is holding me as his prisoner."

"Did you honestly think he would just release you to go about as you pleased, rallying Stephen's forces, when he was on the business of his Empress?"

A frown marred her brow at the thought of what she would have done if their situations had been reversed. "Nay," she replied reluctantly, "I suppose not but he does not understand the importance of why I serve Stephen."

Beatrix finally relaxed back in her chair. "Considering none of us are going anywhere soon, you shall have plenty of time to fill him in."

"'Tis none of his business why I do the things I must," Annora retorted once again angry with herself for being captured in the first place.

"You will soon learn that Richard will make it his business. He is as stubborn as a mule, but he is an honorable man, Lady Annora. Given half a chance, you may even come to favor him."

A sarcastic laugh left her lips. "When hell freezes over!"

A smirk slid across Beatrix's mouth. "Well, 'tis awfully cold outside and Stephen *is* starving us to death with his siege so we may be closer to hell than you think."

Annora watched as Beatrix stood and went to the bed where several gowns were laid out for her to choose from. "I am not wearing any of those," she said firmly.

Beatrix looked back over her shoulder. "Any one of these should fit you. I selected them myself from my own wardrobe and from those of the other ladies in waiting who are still here."

Annora shook her head. "Absolutely not. My own garments are perfectly suitable considering my situation."

Beatrix went over to the clothes that had been carelessly tossed onto the floor before her bath. She picked up the tunic and lifted the fabric to her nose and sniffed. She immediately dropped it back into the dirty pile. "I cannot allow you to put those filthy things back on your body. At least not until we can have them laundered."

"Who made you in charge of me?" Annora inquired completely miffed that this woman was telling what she could or could not wear.

"Richard did when he asked me to attend you… at least until you are returned to his company," Beatrix answered heading back over to the bed and picking out a gown that reminded Annora of autumn.

"I am certain I am much older than you are and am perfectly capable of making my own decisions on what I should wear," Annora declared folding her arms over her chest.

Beatrix lifted one delicate brow. "Your judgement must be severely impaired if you plan on wearing those foul-smelling garments when there are other options available. As to my age, I am a score and four, not that it should matter."

She *was* younger than Annora, though not as young as she had supposed. "And not as yet married." That seemed surprising. The woman was quite beautiful, and from the richness of her gowns,

Annora doubted she lacked for fortune.

A sigh escaped the younger lady. "Do not remind me. My brother does so often enough that I am tempted to run away with the first eligible man who might make me happy."

"Like the one who stood guard at the door?"

Beatrix turned with the gown draped over her arm. "Aye. Exactly so, but do not think you have succeeded in distracting me from the inevitable. Let us get you dressed. This gown will look lovely on you."

Annora's turned her eyes toward her own garments left on the floor. As much as she wished to cling to the familiarity they represented, she had to admit that she could not remember the last time she had been able to wash them. Aye… she had very little desire to put the tunic and hose back on now that she had been allowed the luxury of a bath. Dressing in something so filthy would negate all the benefits of the bath, and there was no telling when she might be allowed another one. She assumed the resources at Oxford Castle were running low. This bath might be her last one for a while.

When had she last been dressed in a gown? Memories of her life with Leofric came into her mind reminding her of happier times. Theirs had been an arranged marriage between their families and they had been virtually strangers at the time when they were wed. Still, she had come to care for her husband, and she missed him dearly, even if she could not honesty say that she had been madly in love with him. He had been appropriately named for he had always reminded her of a lion with his long blondish hair and soft brown eyes. And when their son had been born, Leif had been named after Leofric's sire. They had been happy—a quiet sort of happiness that she'd learned to adjust to over time. There was never any of the passion between them that Annora had always longed for in her marriage, but 'twas a small sacrifice to lay aside those foolish, girlish dreams in favor of a peaceful, contented life. She performed her duties and had given birth to Leofric's heir. Even though he desired more sons, Leif had not been blessed with any further siblings, a situation that had caused some discord in her marriage, putting a wedge between her and her husband that furthered the distance between them.

But Leofric was still fair and had indulged her when she asked to continue her sword play. 'Twas a practice that had carried over since she was quite young, when her own father taught her to defend herself. And whilst the lady of the castle had dressed according to her station in the evenings, she would easily be found in tunic and hose during the days to permit her to move freely during her hours of training. She started to have a reputation as an accomplished swordswoman and Leofric would invite his friends to their home to see if they could best her on the training field. It had pleased her that her husband had been proud of her accomplishments rather than disappointed that she wasn't more ladylike. She had been more than happy to demonstrate her prowess to any and all comers.

Mayhap that had been her downfall in the end. Had she been less eager to show off, less proud of her achievements, word of her skill with the blade might have stayed hidden, and she could have avoided the situation she now found herself in. Her castle had been ransacked. Her husband had fallen in his attempts to protect their home. And her son had been taken hostage whilst she had been forced to serve a man she would never accept as her king. All in all, her life was a shambles and she had no idea how or when she would see her son anytime soon.

Once she was gowned and her hair had been dressed—twisted back neatly in a bun—Beatrix gave her final approval and she was deemed ready to join the others to break their fast. They left the bedchamber and Annora half listened while Beatrix chatted away with some nonsense about her brother's vow to find her a husband and keeping her safe. *Keep her safe?* If this was truly Richard's intent, then Beatrix should be far from her current situation. Annora did not think Richard knew the meaning of keeping someone safe if his sister was being kept here during a siege!

Annora continued to follow Beatrix down the stairs to exit the turret of Oxford Castle. When they reached the great hall, the young woman swept her hand before them as if she were a favored guest being welcomed into their company. *Guest...* she was hardly that, but Annora stepped forward into the room whilst conversations lowered to hushed whispers as all who were gathered stopped to stare. For better or worse, she had the feeling her life had just altered and there was no going back to the way things used to be.

CHAPTER SEVEN

RICHARD'S GAZE SWEPT in avid appreciation over the vision who stood at the entrance to the great hall and almost choked on the ale he was attempting to swallow. If he had any doubts that Annora would be nearly as beautiful in a lovely gown than when he had seen her unclothed, those doubts had now left him. The color suited her well and as she and Beatrix began to make their way into the room, he could not help but be aware of the fine figure she had. The gown itself was the shade of burnt orange that suited her admirably. The white undertunic reached to points on her wrists whilst peeking out at the puffed area at her shoulders and neckline. Jewels were all that was lacking... this woman should have jewels worthy of her adorning her neck and ears.

He shook himself out of the ramblings inside his head when she approached. Beatrix went to a place next to Oswin and the two began to converse in hushed whispers. Richard finally stood to stare directly into the green eyes of the woman who might haunt his dreams for years to come.

"Annora."

"Richard."

He thought she might say more but she remained standing there whilst studying him much as he had just done to her. He motioned to the chair next to him. "Please be seated," he said gruffly. "'Tis not much in the way of a meal but 'tis all we have to offer, and 'twill help to break your fast."

She lifted one brow as he pulled out the chair but not seeing another option, given that all the other seats were taken, she at last moved around the table to sit. He also finally sat before pushing a bowl of porridge closer to her. When she reached for a spoon at the same time, their fingers briefly touched. Annora gasped even whilst a zing of currents raced up his arm. *Bloody hell!* Had it really been that long since he had a woman that the first one he touched would set his skin afire?

She quickly pulled back her hand and he swore he could still imagine the heat of her skin next to his own. He once again pushed the utensil in her direction and she at last seemingly composed herself and began to eat. She grimaced at the taste but did not hesitate to eat her fill without complaint, showing an admiral pragmatism that he could only wish his sister would emulate. They ate in silence, with Richard drinking as much as he could until his cup was empty. Annora finished her meal and then gazed about the room.

"You are all starving here," she said, voicing his own troubled thoughts aloud.

He turned in his chair to fully look upon her. "You yourself were a part of laying siege to the city of Oxford and this very castle. Surely this is the result you anticipated. Did you expect anything less when Stephen controls the ports and there is nothing coming into this keep in the way of resources?"

"'Twas not as though I was part of the planning," she said frowning. "I am but following orders much as you are with your Empress."

He was about to answer her when a shriek echoed in the room. Everyone turned their attention to Lady Eden Howlande, who was one of the Empress's ladies in waiting and who had just entered the great hall. The other two, Lady Rovena and Lady Petula, followed closely behind her.

Eden rushed across the room before coming to grip the edges of the table where Richard was seated. "Lord Richard..." she began before leaning forward. "Whatever are you doing here? Where is—"

"The last I saw her, she was being ushered away with Norwood and the other knights," he replied as he interrupted her, keeping her from saying too much in front of Annora.

"Without you?" Eden asked but then frowned at the stranger sitting next to him.

"There was a... complication."

"Complication?"

"Aye. An unforeseen one," Richard answered still not giving the irate woman any further information.

"And who is this?" Eden finally asked.

"The complication," Richard replied glancing at Annora who did not bother to hide her displeasure at being characterized in this way.

Annora dropped her spoon into the bowl. "I have a voice or am I not allowed to use it?" she snapped.

Richard waved his hand toward Eden. "By all means. Feel free to voice your grievances to the lady."

"You are the rudest man I have ever had the displeasure to meet," Annora said instead.

"And you are not exactly behaving like a typical demure lady either," Richard declared with a smirk.

"How dare you?" Annora said slamming her fist upon the table.

"I have the feeling I will be daring much in the coming months if we shall continue to be forced into close proximity with one another, Annora."

"Months?" she bellowed. "You cannot hold me against my will for months, Richard!"

A chuckle left him. "Watch me."

They stared at one another and 'twas as though he could see her mentally counting the options before her. For all her stubbornness, she must see that there were not many.

Lady Eden cleared her throat. "If the two of you are done squabbling about your differences, would you care to fill me in on what is going on here?"

Richard gave a heavy sigh. "May I present Lady Annora de Maris. This is Lady Eden Howlande, Lady Rovena Eatone, and Lady Petula Wintere. They are the ladies in waiting to Empress Matilda," Richard announced as he waved his hand down the table to his sister. "As is Beatrix, my sister, whom you have obviously already met."

Annora nodded her head. "Ladies…"

"What have you done, Richard?" Eden finally asked.

"Done? I have done nothing but to ensure Empress Matilda was able to continue onward with her plans after we were interrupted by someone who could have warned Stephen's soldiers of the Empress's escape. When she stumbled upon us as we were crossing through Stephen's camp, what else was I to do but take the lady hostage?"

"But you are one of Empress Matilda's most trusted knights. How could she go on without you?" Eden inquired.

"I am but one of many, Lady Eden. She is well guarded by Norwood, Kennarde, and Goodee. I am certain the Empress made her way across the river without further incident and even now is making her way to safety."

Eden gave a sigh of relief. "Then I will continue to pray this will soon all be over."

The three women left to take their usual places at the head table where the Empress's chair remained empty for obvious reasons.

"You cannot hold me here for months. I have obligations—serious ones. A life is at stake," Annora continued in a low voice after the women had left.

"At last, a hint of honesty in your words. How refreshing."

"I was honest when I said you were the rudest man I have ever encountered," she muttered, a mulish expression on her face.

In spite of himself, Richard chuckled. "Aye, I'd wager you were."

"This is hardly a joke," she retorted, beginning to look genuinely upset. She attempted to hold back a sob, but Richard could see the tears that hinted at leaking from her eyes. "You know nothing of my life nor the obligations that cause me to do the things I must."

"Then tell me of them so I might form some bit of sympathy for you, if such a thing is possible considering you are in service to my enemy," Richard said waiting for her reply so he might at least try to understand her motives.

"Nay. I will not tell you anything that you will hold against me. Throw me into the dungeon or the castle pit for all I care but as far as you are concerned, I am nothing but a prisoner under your thumb."

Annora's chair loudly scraped against the stone floor and the dirty rushes as she rose to her feet. She did not wait for a reply but instead, she raised her chin and left the hall to return, he assumed, to their bedchamber. Richard closely followed behind, afraid if she reached the room before him, she'd slide the bolt home against him and he'd be left to fend for himself in the cold passageway.

CHAPTER EIGHT

Annora expected to leave the hall alone with whatever remained of her dignity. But apparently, she had thought wrong. When she entered the turret and looked behind her, she saw Richard close behind. Damn him! She wanted to take the curved stairs two at a time in order to escape him, but while that might have been possible if she were dressed in her usual hose and tunic, there was too much fabric to this dress to move quickly. It caught between her legs until she finally lifted the gown up above her knees and hastened her steps.

Richard did the same. "Annora!"

Her name called out in that deep baritone caused her body to shiver in unexpected delight. Nay! She would not give in to any feelings of attraction toward the beast who held her against her will. Instead, she would separate herself from his company completely. When she reached the floor to the bedchamber they shared, she sprinted down the passageway toward the open door that was like a beacon offering her safety, if only she could reach it in time.

She darted inside the room and went to slam the wooden portal shut as quickly as she could. She had been so close to ensuring her privacy for the day but clearly Richard was just as fast as he, too, pushed against the portal preventing her from sealing it shut. She was no match for his strength, and she finally gave up struggling against him. Letting go of the door, the wood slammed against the wall whilst Richard filled the room. He was like a dark lion on the prowl as he quickly closed the distance between them. But she had no mind to be caught in his grasp as she put first the table between them and then a chair as he followed her around the room that felt as if 'twas getting smaller by the second. The chair soon bounced to the floor when he easily knocked it out of his way and closed in on her, grabbing hold of her shoulders.

She was pulled against that firm chest of muscles. Rock hard like a marble statue, she could even feel the ripples of his stomach and she knew his body, if fully revealed, would show him to be every inch the warrior.

"You will be the death of me, woman," he scolded. But despite the aggravation in his tone, she thought she heard a hint of unspoken desire as well. Surely, she must be imaging such a happening.

"I could not be that lucky," she hotly retorted.

"Do you never have anything kind to say?" he asked pulling her closer causing her to lift her hands to push against his solid chest. He did not budge even an inch.

A short laugh escaped her lips. "To you? The man who is holding me against my will? I think not."

"Perchance I can change your mind so we can find a common accord between us." God help her, but his tone was like that of a lover. Had it really been so long since she had a man in her bed that the first one to come along who held her this close had only to murmur a few suggestive words in order to wreak havoc with her heart?

"I will never be amicable to anything you might offer," she declared instead of giving voice to this sudden, forbidden attraction. 'Twas clear that her heart would betray her, but her mind remained her own, and she would not allow herself to be swayed into giving any quarter to this man.

"I have heard that one should never say never, dearest Annora," he said in another purely sinful tone. When he reached up to brush a lock of her hair back, she swore her heart flipped end over end.

"I am *not* your dearest," she snarled trying to catch her breath, "and you are not man enough to convince me to change my mind about the conclusions I have drawn as to your character."

His smile broadened across his handsome features. "From the look of you, I believe you speak a falsehood, my lady. Why, if I did not know better, I would say from your heaving bosom and your attempts to breathe normally that you might even desire me just a little."

"Desire you? You must be mad," she lied trying to push against his chest again to no avail. "I can barely stand being in your presence, Grancourt."

"You will be hard pressed to keep your distance given the proximity we will be forced into due to the size of this bedchamber. And while I may guard the door, a man can only stand the floor for so long before he longs for his own bed."

"Then let me go and you may return to sleeping in your bed very much alone."

A chuckle rumbled in his chest. "By Saint Michael's wings, I somehow think I like the banter between us."

"Banter? Do you find my captivity to be an appropriate matter to jest about? I would hate you for that alone, even if I did not hate you already."

"There is a fine line between hate and love… or so I have heard since the emotion of loving someone has never consumed me. But let us prove this theory you have put forward that you are indifferent to me," he said with a roguish grin.

"Do not dare—"

"Oh, but I think I must. You are too tempting not to taste those lips that are ripe for kissing."

"Do not think I will permit you to kiss me," she growled, but he seemed anything but deterred by her warning.

"I do so enjoy a challenge," he said cutting off her words before she could make any reply as he leaned forward to slide his mouth slowly over the seam of her lips.

This simple act was so sensual that her knees immediately buckled beneath her, and Richard tightened his grip around her waist to keep her from falling. His mouth teased hers, waiting for her to open up to the possibilities he was offering, tempting her to give in to his exploring. She kept her lips tightly pressed together until she felt a gentle nibble of his teeth on her lower lip. 'Twas playful in a way that she had never experienced before, and she found herself unable to suppress her response. Her gasp gave him the freedom to plunge forward as his mouth took full possession of hers.

And possess her he did whilst every fiber of her being melted as though all the blood rushing through her veins were on fire. A moan escaped her caused the man holding her to clutch her even more tightly in his arms, pressing his body fully into hers whilst his tongue danced a rhythm with hers known to lovers throughout all time. His fingers tangled in her hair and the bun that Beatrix had coiffed came undone. The tawny length flowed down her back and was gripped in fists that tugged deliciously, even as Richard continued to assault her very senses. Annora was lost and she cared not that any words she had flung in Richard's direction were now proven to be a complete lie. What was the point of spouting such falsehoods when he would know the truth of the matter the moment his lips left hers?

'Twas as though he read her thoughts for those startling blue eyes opened to stare upon her with what she thought was fascination. He appeared as though he was just as surprised as she was by her reaction to his kiss. His mouth lingered next to her own... their breath mingling together on a heartbeat. She could have sworn her very soul called out to his as if she had finally found her match for the passion she had always carried in her heart. This sensation was what she had once hoped to find with her husband—a feeling she had given up on finding at all. And yet here it was, with this man she had been determined to despise forever.

He pushed back some of her tresses and the palm of his hand

cupped her cheek. "It appears, my dearest Annora, that you are not as indifferent to me as you might claim," Richard whispered before he placed another quick kiss upon her swollen, sensitive lips.

He let her go and she almost stumbled without his support. She quickly recovered herself and went to right the chair that had been knocked over. There were no words she could say, not when her heart had yet to recover from the passionate intensity of his embrace. She felt as unsteady as if she stood aboard a ship sailing through storm-tossed seas, but she struggled not to show it. He must not know how deeply she was affected. Richard went to a table and picked up a book taking it over to the alcove where a comfortable cushion was placed so he could read by the window.

Relieved that his attention was no longer focused upon her, Annora all but fell into the chair near the hearth whilst her heart at last began to slow. As she stared at the knight who now appeared engrossed in his book, she could only wonder how she could make her escape before the urges of her body fully overpowered the reasoning of her mind. She could not afford to become infatuated with this man, or to crave his touch. Not when her son's life depended on her returning to Stephen's camp.

Annora knew if she did not leave soon, she would be in trouble. The longer she stayed, the more she might be tempted to let her guard down and this was something she could not afford. She had to keep this man from gaining any further influence over her. Her only concern should be her son, who needed her.

The hours ticked by. The day slowly progressed. Having nothing to do to occupy her mind, she could have sworn her heart was asking her with ever beat it took *what if... what if... what if...*

CHAPTER NINE

RICHARD LIFTED HIS sword and the blade struck Oswin's with a loud clang. The inner bailey was filled with knights who continued to train despite the hunger that gnawed at their bellies. Richard had insisted the men continue with the maneuvers that would see them fit to fight another day against Stephen. Such an outcome could come any day although Richard prayed that word would soon reach their enemy that Empress Matilda was no longer inside the castle. Afterwards, there would be no need for Stephen to continue to hold its people under siege. Not when the main reason that motivated the siege was no longer in residence. Richard would still love to see the usurper's reaction when he was given the news that the Empress had evaded capture yet again.

But that day had yet to come, and the inhabitants of Oxford Castle continued to hold out, not daring to allow word to spread to Stephen's camp of the Empress's absence for fear that he might be able to capture her if he sent men after her before she was able to reach safety. Nay, in order to give the Empress adequate time to escape, 'twas his duty to keep Stephen in the dark for as long as possible. Richard knew the going would be difficult. If they crossed the river without the ice cracking, then the Empress's party had six miles to travel on foot in the middle of winter. The plan had been for her to procure horses in Abingdon and then ride on to her vassal Brian fitzCount's manor in Wallingford.

Once rested, Empress Matilda and the rest of her party would eventually make their way to Devizes Castle. The castle once belonged to her father Henry I and would be the perfect place to fully recover from their travels. The place was as secure as Oxford and Richard had no doubt Empress Matilda would one day reside here again. 'Twas only a matter of time, and given the obstacles she might face on the journey, 'twas Richard's wish to ensure that she had as much time as possible, at any cost to himself.

The past few days had been sheer torture keeping himself confined in his bedchamber with Annora sitting close by. Few words had been spoken since he had done the unthinkable. Kissing her had been a mistake. She had made it perfectly clear that she wanted no part of him, and he could hardly blame her. How often must he remind himself that he had made her a prisoner and that therefore an unsurmountable rift lay between them? Obviously several more, because despite his many attempts in the past few days to have speech with her on even the most mundane, pedestrian concerns of their situation, he could never break the icy barrier she put in place between them—and he could never stop *wanting* to break that barrier. Fool that he was, he longed to be closer to the woman who seemed to hold him in nothing but disdain.

He swung his blade again taking his frustration out on Oswin who finally stepped back and sheathed his sword.

"Bloody hell, Richard!" he fumed. "What the devil is bothering you that you must needs take out your anger on me?"

Richard shook his head to clear it and then also put his sword inside the scabbard at his side. "My apologies, Oswin. As you can tell, I am in a foul mood."

Oswin continued to frown whilst inspecting him. "All is forgiven but does your anger have anything to do with a certain lady you hold captive?"

Richard rolled his eyes causing Oswin's laughter to ring out in the yard. "If you only knew the half of it."

Oswin came and placed his hand upon Richard's shoulder. "Women... they are a nuisance in our lives, but we cannot live without them either. Yours, in particular, would be hard to erase from your mind since she is ever near."

"I could hardly put her in the dungeon," Richard said scowling whilst mentally wondering if Oswin's words were an indication of the status of whatever his relationship with Beatrix was.

"Nay. I suppose you could not but certainly you could have assigned her another chamber to sleep in besides your own."

Richard raked his hand through his hair. "And then have to stand guard outside her door? Nay. She is better off in my own chamber where I can keep a closer eye on her."

Oswin chuckled again. "If you say so, but I do not know how you are managing to hold on to your peace of mind. She is a very beautiful woman."

Richard heaved a sigh. "I will not deny that she has occupied much of my thoughts of late."

"And occupied your bed as well," Oswin pointed out slyly.

"That she has—*alone*. 'Tis not as if I share it with her."

"Is there not room enough for you both?"

Richard scowled at the suggestion. "I do not make it a habit of taking a woman who is not of a like mind, and she would sooner welcome a rattlesnake into her arms. If you have not noticed, Annora hates me."

"Does she really? Mayhap you have not noticed how her eyes follow you around the room then when you are not paying any attention to her," Oswin mentioned whilst crossing his arms over his chest.

Richard raised his head to stare at his friend. "I hardly believe she is interested in me beyond her plotting as to how she might escape my presence or plunge a knife in my back."

Oswin shrugged and bent slightly over to stare behind Richard.

"Well, we are about to find out since she appears to be ready to train with you or one of the men."

Richard whirled around and his cape wrapped around his legs as he spun. He pulled the offensive garment away to stare in wonder at the woman who approached. God's wounds but she was incredible, and her hose and tunic peeking out from her own brown cape as she crossed the bailey. She was back in her old attire, which had been laundered and mended, and he did not know if he liked her better in a dress or the hose that outlined her shapely legs. Either one seemed to suit her obscenely well. She boldly came to stand before him and began tapping her boot.

"I would like the return of my sword so that I might train with your men," she demanded gazing up at him with those green eyes. He swore this woman was going to bewitch him at any moment.

"I think not," Richard answered as he crossed the yard to where a tankard was waiting for him. He picked up the cup and took a drink before setting it back down on the stone bench.

Annora had, of course, followed him. "Afraid I might beat you at your swordplay?"

A snort left his lips at the thought. "Hardly."

"Then what scares you, Grancourt? I would think it would give you a fair amount of satisfaction to beat a mere woman."

"There is nothing about you, Annora, that I consider simple," Richard proclaimed but inside he was thoroughly amused by her gall. She had gumption and he certainly appreciated the fact that she had no issue standing up to him.

She must have been caught off guard by his reaction, considering her startled expression. No doubt she had viewed her taunt as the sort of challenge no man would endure, and his calmness had rattled her. But she recovered herself quickly and continued to press the issue. "Then there should be no point in not allowing me to train. 'Tis of import or else you would not have the men out here in this nasty weather to see that they, too, remain fit."

He considered her for a few minutes, then reached inside the pouch on his belt and tossed Oswin a key. "Oswin… would you be so good as to retrieve the lady's sword? You'll find her blade inside the chest at the foot of my bed in my bedchamber."

Oswin laughed. "Are you certain, Richard?"

"Go," Richard answered with a nod of his head, never taking his eyes from the lady.

Oswin left and came back several minutes later. He handed the sword to Annora who began to swing the familiar blade before her.

"Shall we, Grancourt?" she asked stepping back and taking up her stance.

He inspected her whilst taking hold of the hilt of his sword. Lifting the blade from the scabbard, he rested the blade on his shoulder. "Are you certain you are up to the task, Annora?"

A sound much like a baited animal left her as she lunged forward. Her mistake was letting all her pent-up anger get the better of her. She swung her blade recklessly and Richard easily deflected her sword without any injury incurring even though she did her best to pierce his body.

Over and over did she make an attempt to inflict some sort of harm to him but because she was not thinking clearly, none of her blows were able to deal any damage. 'Twas not long before her energy began to run out and Richard could see for himself that she did not have much left to give, and yet she refused to give way. Snow began to fall in earnest and the ground became slippery and still she fought on.

"Yield, Annora. The men and I will not think less of you or your techniques," Richard said offering her a form of truce.

"Nay, you mindless cur. You are the reason everything I hold dear is in jeopardy," she yelled back and continued her onslaught to win the day.

Blinded with rage, her chest heaved as she took in huge gulps of air. Richard could plainly see that if she did not stop soon, she would not only hurt herself but mayhap someone else as well. He had had enough.

He attacked her relentlessly if only to prove his point. Backing her up caused her to lose her footing and she slipped on the ice beneath her feet and found herself held at the point of his blade. 'Twas a familiar scene and one that reminded him of when this castle fell to the enemy.

"Yield, Annora," he repeated his words from but moments ago.

She nodded for he did not give her any other choice on the matter. But when he held out his hand to assist her from the ground, she slapped it away.

"I do not need your help, Grancourt." She rose to her feet on her own accord whilst he put his sword away.

"Mayhap not but I think I should claim a reward for beating a fair Viking shield maiden," Richard proclaimed and he quickly reached out to grab her about the waist. He pulled her into his body and before he could think better of what he was about to do, he thoroughly kissed her. He thought perchance she was enjoying herself until he pulled his lips from hers and a slap across the cheek was his own reward. The men began to laugh, though whether their amusement was from watching Richard take possession of the lady or from Annora's self-righteous anger with her physical reply to his kiss, he could not say.

She backed away from him and pointed her finger at him. "Never—and I repeat *never*—steal another kiss from me without my permission or you shall pay the consequences," she warned.

"Such an action may be worth it," Richard teased but inside wondered what was coming over him. He was never this reckless with a woman's affection and to be holding one in such an embrace without her consent went against his sense of honor.

"You have been warned."

She was about to leave but Richard again took hold of her arm.

"Not so fast, Annora," Richard said as he stared down into those mesmerizing green eyes. "I believe you forgot to return your sword."

Her lips pursed and Richard could only think about tasting her once again. She at last held out her blade for him to take. "Damn you to hell, Richard," she replied before she stomped off to return to the keep.

Richard stared after the woman as she left before he turned his attention to her sword. He rubbed his thumb over the hilt where there was an indent where a jewel must have once been placed. *Green... there should be an emerald there that would match her eyes*, he thought knowing he would need to see the smithy to rectify the matter.

Richard rubbed at his cheek and could still feel the heat from the imprint she most likely left on his face. 'Twas as though she had branded him. *God... what a woman!*

CHAPTER TEN

Annora held her composure until she was out of sight of the men. Once she was fully away from the area where they trained, she crumbled onto the ground hugging her knees as she allowed despair to overwhelm her. She laid her head down on her knees to choke back the tears threatening to fall from her eyes. She had never let someone get under her skin before—had always been careful never to fight with anger ruling her head. But something about that man provoked her beyond measure, until any form of training she had had in the past flew out of her mind. Her only thought was to take out her frustrations on Richard. *He* was the reason everything in her life was a complete mess.

And then that kiss… if she had allowed him to continue she might have done the unthinkable and actually given in to the pleasure he aroused in her. Leofric had never kissed her like that and mayhap 'twas the reason she never felt anything for him beyond affection. A heavy sigh left her as she contemplated her life of old. 'Twas not exactly how she had imagined her life, but many marriages came with much less. She and her husband had a common accord and mutual respect. She had lived her life with him and was grateful he gave her a fair amount of freedom to do as she pleased.

But Richard… he could be something far more dangerous to her heart if she let him in. The possibility was there. No matter the harsh words they may spout at one another, there was an underlying amount of passion that continued to rear its ugly head whenever the opportunity took over. His handsome face and strong body stirred an attraction in her like none she had ever known, but the feelings growing in her breast went beyond simple lust. Over the past several days, she had watched him and she could not discount the fact that he appeared as though he cared for those who were attempting to survive the circumstances they found themselves in. He was more honorable than she would ever admit aloud—not to mention brave, strong, commanding. It all served to make him even more appealing, damn him.

But where did this leave her? Her son was still held by Stephen's men back at her home at Meregate Castle. Her obligations to Stephen continued to hang over her head, and she had begun to fear he would never release her from her service to him. But why *was* he so determined to keep her under his command? 'Twas not as though he did not have others who were capable of fighting on his behalf. In fact, if she were honest with herself, as a woman, the strength of her arm was no match for a man's. Against inexperienced soldiers, she could well hold her own, due to her training and the tricks she had learned to use her opponents' size against them. But against a man who was well trained, she would inevitably tire or weaken first.

So why was Stephen so insistent on having her fight under his banner? The only thing she could ever think of was that Stephen valued her home due to Meregate's location. A seaport, it would provide another place where Stephen's ships could land in the event he invaded from the sea. With her away, and his men stationed within her home to monitor her son, Stephen could use that port as he pleased. It made sense, not that he ever divulged such reasoning. Had he permitted her to stay at home with her son, she'd have allowed him free use of the port—but instead, he'd chosen to drag her way and to hold her son captive. That in itself was cause to view him as her enemy no matter she had to fight for his cause.

Would Richard be sympathetic to the reason she fought for King

Stephen? She could confide all to him and perchance he might help her liberate her son and her home once Oxford was no longer under siege. Could she trust him? She shook her head not knowing the answer, her heart filled with worry and confusion over how she was beginning to feel for the man. She had only been in his company for a short while. How could she have feelings for the man this soon? She barely knew him and had no idea how to handle this growing desire for her enemy.

And if her feelings continued to grow into something much greater than mere desire…then that would be more dangerous still.

She knew he stood above her before she even raised her head. His hand was held out for her to take.

"Come, Annora," Richard offered softly. "You shall catch a cold if you stay upon the frozen ground much longer."

This time, her gloved hand slid easily into his and he gave a gentle tug to help her rise to her feet. His thumb ran over the back of her fingers whilst he continued to hold onto her quaking limb. She was unsure if she was uneasy because of her earlier thoughts of him or what it could mean to her son if she stayed. Either way her emotions were getting the better of her.

"Thank you," she murmured before raising her head to stare into his blue eyes. She wanted to brush back a lock of his black hair that had fallen rakishly over his forehead, but she resisted the temptation. The harsh scowl that seemed to crease his forehead whenever they had another argument was gone. Instead, he offered her a small smile of encouragement that seemed to entreat her to trust him.

"You are most welcome," he said kindly before tucking her hand into the crook of his elbow. He began escorting her back into the keep where he made his way to the hearth. With their limited supplies, the fire there would barely take the chill from most of the room but he moved a chair closer to its warmth so she would benefit the most from its meager heat. Once she was seated, he pulled a second chair directly next to hers and took her hands again.

"Tell me what is troubling you, Annora, so I might better understand your plight. I am not the ogre you think I am," he began with what sounded like a sincere heart.

"I never said you were a monster," she retorted before turning her head away from him. His tone seemed so honest and another piece of ice she had built to surround her heart cracked. But apparently he was not done with her yet for he reached out to gently turn her head so he might see her completely. His blue eyes felt as though they probed down into the very depth of her soul.

"Tell me," he whispered softly. His tone was so sincere she could not doubt he honestly wished to know her plight. Her heart split wide open.

"I have a son…" A cry left her lips and she buried her head in her hands.

He pulled her into his lap and she wound her arms around him as she sobbed out her heartache. How long had it been since arms had held her close to offer her comfort? Perchance from Merek after her husband had been killed but it had been briefly, and she certainly had not felt the same amount of relief in her captain's arms as she felt now in Richard's embrace.

"I did not realize you were married," he said stroking her hair."

"I am a widow."

"I am sorry for your loss, but I will admit I am relieved I have not coveted another man's wife," Richard replied placing a kiss upon the side of her brow.

She raised her head to stare at him with tear-streaked cheeks. She brushed the moisture from her face with her sleeve not knowing what to say until the words burst unbidden from her lips. "You want me?"

He gave her a crooked smile. "As no doubt you could surmise. Rest assured that 'tis not my habit to force myself upon a lady and steal her kisses without permission. I apologize if I hurt or distressed you, but in truth, the attraction I feel for you has made me struggle to behave as a gentleman."

Her hand automatically covered her mouth even whilst she came to the realization she was playing with the end of a strand of his hair with the other. "I give you leave to do so now," she murmured without thinking of the consequences.

One of his dark brows rose at her words. "And what if I want more from you than just your kisses?"

She could not help herself when she widened her eyes. He could easily take her but she might bear the burden of their coupling if she were to get pregnant. She reached over to cup his cheek and he took hold of her hand to place a kiss at the inside of her wrist.

"I do not have the freedom to give you more of myself, Richard," she said finally answering him. "I have obligations that must come first, and those commitments are to my son."

He lowered his head in thought before raising his eyes to gaze upon her again. His smile this time was as though a piece of his heart was also breaking that they had no future together. But mayhap she only imagined the grief in his eyes since 'twas what she was feeling. His words almost confirmed her thoughts.

"I, too, am not free to offer you all that you deserve, Annora. My service is firmly placed with the Empress Matilda's cause and until she releases me, I am her most humble vassal."

Annora nodded and decided to confide in him. "My husband was killed during a siege by Stephen's men. Meregate Castle is on the coast north of Dover. My guess is Stephen wished to have control of the port. He had learned of my ability with a sword for my husband Leofric was one to boast of my accomplishments and taunt his friends into seeing if they could beat me at swordplay. Stephen compelled me to join his forces, and he continues to hold my son, Leif, hostage in order to control me."

"That is why you fight for the usurper," Richard stated whilst running his finger down her cheek.

"Aye. If I remain his warrior to fight for his cause, he assures my son's survival. I would not be lending him my sword arm for any other reason. I continue to think of Stephen as my enemy because of everything he has cost me, but I must obey his commands," Annora replied softly.

"Perchance once Oxford is again free from his clutches, I might petition the Empress to help you regain your home and son," Richard offered as he once again stroked her hair.

"Why would you make such an offer? You do not owe me anything and we barely know one another," she asked.

"Mayhap I wish we could be more to each other one day than enemies fighting on opposites sides of this war."

A slight laugh left her. "The world would have to completely change for such a miracle to occur," she teased and suddenly realized she was still sitting on his lap. She tried to rise but he held her firmly in place. "What will people think if they see me like this?"

"I do not care what others think."

She tore her gaze from his and saw that the hall remained empty. Instead of arguing with him, she took advantage of the situation. Another one might never occur, and she wanted this one moment unto herself. "Then kiss me, Richard. Just this once, let me feel what 'tis like to be desired as a woman."

"I thought you would never ask," he said in a tone that caused Annora to shiver in delight.

She pressed lightly at the back of his neck until their lips were but inches apart. Yet still he waited until her patience reached an end. This time 'twas Annora who initiated their kiss. She wound her arms around his neck whilst she took complete control. She supposed she should end this, and she knew that Richard would never deny her the right to pull away, but she had no notion to do so. Instead, she poured every ounce of energy into satisfying her hunger for this man. He more than proved he desired her as much as she wanted him. If only they had met in some other place and time…

For once in her life, Annora gave in to the sensation of being wanted for herself. Richard made her feel safe for the first time in months. She became completely lost, and Richard was the only man who could save her.

CHAPTER ELEVEN

RICHARD PACED THE passageway outside of his bedchamber. Annora was inside changing into her hose and tunic. He did not care for what was about to transpire downstairs in the great hall, but what choice did they have? And yet, even though he should have known all along that this was how things would end, his heart rebelled against it. He did not wish to release Annora so that she could return to the man who had such a cruel hold over her. He wished 'twas possible for her to stay by his side, always. They had come to a common accord in the past several days and had been enjoying each other's company. But all that was about to change, and Richard did not know how to alter the situation. He would be forced to let her go.

The afternoon had brought a messenger carrying a white flag to the gates of Oxford and bearing Stephen's missive. The parchment had been brought to Richard and after he broke the wax seal, he perused its contents briefly. He then began issuing orders to allow Stephen to enter the gate and to make him comfortable in the great hall. 'Twas clear the usurper had learned of the Empress's escape. There was nothing left to do but surrender the castle and pray that any terms would be amicable.

His bedchamber door opened. Annora was in the process of placing one of her knives he had originally taken from her into one of her boots. She finally stood and he could see for himself her worried frown. He came inside and pulled her into his arms. "I wish there was another way to keep you with me," Richard said brushing away the tears that escaped her green eyes.

"I wish I could stay," she whispered before continuing, "but we knew this day would come eventually."

"We were just starting to like one another," he teased with a short chuckle to lighten the mood.

"Imagine what might have been with a bit more time," she declared with a smile that did not reach her worried eyes.

Richard sighed. "I have imagined such a life every night, Annora."

"You have?" she asked.

"Aye. I wish there was a way that we could continue what has begun between us and find out if we could suit long term."

She tore herself out of his arms and made her way further into the room. "You should not make this any more difficult than it already is, Richard. You know what is at stake for me. I must return to my duties with Stephen for the sake of my son."

"Aye, I understand. I do not take pleasure in losing you, though."

"We always knew our situation would come to this," she repeated with a shake of her head. "My son must take priority over anything else I might personally desire."

"So, you do desire me? I had my doubts on many an occasion since we first met," Richard replied with a crooked smile.

"I will not add to the conceit inside your head and declare when everything changed between us in my mind."

"I promise I will find you again," Richard vowed coming back to her and taking her hands. He raised them to his lips.

"I cannot in good faith ask you to make such a vow, Richard. Who knows how long I might have to raise my sword for Stephen's cause?"

"I still willingly make my pledge to you, Annora. I swear to you I *will* find you again."

She gave him a weak smile. "Then I will hold such a promise close to my heart in the months to come."

He pulled her into his arms again and bent forward to kiss her knowing it might indeed be months before their paths crossed again. He prayed his kiss conveyed his unspoken words, and that she knew that he had come to deeply care for her, no matter they had only just met. They tore apart when the door burst open and Beatrix stood there appearing as if she, too, were shaken to her core.

"He asks for everyone to assemble in the hall," Beatrix proclaimed before turning back to Oswin, who waited for her in the passageway. She took his arm and disappeared down the corridor leaving the portal open.

Richard tucked Annora's hand into the crook of his arm and they began making their way through the passageway, down the turret stairs, and then into the great hall. They had a brief moment of surprise seeing Stephen reclining in the Empress's chair, but perchance this told them all they needed to know. Stephen now oversaw Oxford Castle, and they needed to bend the knee in submission.

Richard quickly told Annora to blend in with the others who had gathered in the hall. When he passed a lad, he bent down to whisper an order into his ear. The boy took off whilst Richard strode forward. He bowed before Stephen.

"Your Majesty," Richard said as he then stared into the eyes of the self-proclaimed king.

"You are Lord Richard Grancourt?" King Stephen inquired in a low drawl.

"I am," Richard replied shortly as he waited for the terms of their surrender.

"If I remember correctly your lands are north to those of Wymar Norwood and Brockenhurst. In Lyndhurst, I believe..." the King prodded, waiting for Richard to confirm the location of his lands.

"Aye."

"You are not much for words, Grancourt, but then I suppose you are more concerned for the well-being of those left behind when the Empress fled and deserted you."

"Empress Matilda would wish to ensure that her people were kept safe, Your Majesty," Richard answered.

King Stephen gave a snort of disdain. "How she managed her escape in the first place is still a mystery but there is nothing that can be done about that event at this point."

"What are your terms, Your Highness?" Richard asked.

"'Tis enough that you have bowed down to your rightful ruler in these trying times. You and the others all may return to your normal duties. My terms would have been different if Matilda was still here," Stephen said. His reply startled Richard, who had believed that he would ask for far more.

"Oxford's people will be thankful to know that they are free and the blockade in the harbor shall be lifted," Richard replied with a bow of acknowledgment.

A knight standing behind the King bent down to whisper in his ear causing Stephen's attention to flit around the room until his gaze landed on the one he sought. "There is but one restriction that must needs be adhered to," the King declared loudly for everyone present to hear.

"And that is?" Richard asked already knowing in his heart what would transpire.

Stephen pointed toward the back of the hall. "That woman belongs to me," he proclaimed coming to stand. "Lady de Maris, step forward."

Richard could do nothing more than step aside when Annora made her way to kneel before the king.

"Your Majesty," she said softly keeping her head bowed.

"You gave us quite the fright, Lady de Maris. The captain of your guard was concerned for your welfare," the King said as he stepped forward. He took her chin—inspecting her for signs of abuse, or so Richard supposed.

"As you can see, I am well," Annora said rising to her feet.

"'Tis good that you have not been harmed, although I expected you to be residing in the dungeon and not living among the others."

"I have been treated with the utmost curtesy, my liege," Annora answered, giving a short glance in Richard's direction.

"Very well. We shall work out the rest of the particulars in the coming days. In the meantime, I will have food brought into the castle in order to feed your people, Grancourt," Stephen proclaimed before he began to make his way from the hall.

A man stepped toward Annora and Richard's hand went to the hilt of his sword until the lady gave the man a hug. She then turned to Richard. "This is Merek Baringar who was my Captain of the Guard when we were home at Meregate. Merek, may I present Lord Richard Grancourt of Lyndhurst."

"My lord," Merek muttered before turning to Annora. "Is he the one who took you?"

"We can discuss this later," Annora warned. Obediently, the man backed off whilst Stephen called for them to leave with him.

Richard looked toward the entrance to the hall and saw the lad he had sent off earlier had returned. He gave the lady a smile. Richard waved the boy forward and Annora's sword was placed in Richard's hand. He took to one knee, bowed his head, and held out the blade with both hands.

"I believe this belongs to you, my lady," Richard said, offering her the sword.

"Thank you, Richard," she answered taking the blade and a gasp escaped her when she saw an emerald had been placed in the hilt. "When did you do this?"

"I saw the stone was missing and took the initiative to see that it was replaced. I hope you approve of my choice," Richard stated waiting for her reply.

"'Tis lovely. How can I ever thank you? This gem was surely costly."

Richard stood. He took her hand and lifted her fingertips to his lips. "One day when we meet again, we shall think of something," he said in a husky whisper.

Richard swore her eyes were sparkling in delight. "I shall look forward to our reunion in some other place and time."

She surprised him when she came forward and offered him a hug. His arms wrapped briefly around her waist, and he leaned down to whisper in her ear. "I *will* find you again, Annora."

She quickly released herself from his embrace and he could only watch her nod her head before she left his side. But 'twas the one tear that slid down her cheek that would be etched in his memory in the months to come.

CHAPTER TWELVE

ANNORA STOOD BACK whilst the men took down the last of her tent. Poles were stacked inside a wagon, and, with an expertise that proved that this task had been done more than once, the fabric began to be folded by several knights. She lifted her satchel over her shoulder and made her way to her horse that Merek held for her.

She waved Merek away as she went to tie her satchel to the saddle and began checking the cinches to ensure all were secure. 'Twas nothing more than a habit, for she knew Merek would have seen to such things. He had been overseeing her welfare for many a year and now was no different. She was thankful for his service and the reminder that he remained faithful to her household.

She ran her hands over the black fur of her horse until she took the reins. She patted his muzzle and received what she perceived as a smile until he flapped his lips. Annora laughed knowing all he wished for was a treat. She reached inside her cloak and pulled out an apple that had survived the winter. She held the red fruit beneath his mouth as he began to munch on the unexpected delicacy.

"You are beyond spoiled, Shadow. Are you ready to see where we are off to next?" she asked not expecting a reply but still pleased when he began bobbing his head as though in answer. Placing her foot in the stirrup, she swung herself up onto her horse and settled herself in the saddle as Merek came abreast of her on his own steed.

"Are you ready, Lady de Maris?" Merek inquired as he waved his hand behind him to the others.

"Why so formal an address, Merek?" she asked, before startling at the sudden sound of others coming up behind her. They began to form around Annora like a protective barrier. She turned in the saddle to look at the knights whilst the men kept a steady gaze ahead. "Are we expecting an ambush?"

"I will take no further chances when it comes to your wellbeing, my lady. I failed you once and will not do so again."

"You hardly failed me, Merek," she said with a soft sigh as she focused her attention on her captain. "'Twas certainly not your fault I left my tent in the middle of the night to fall right into our enemy's hands."

Merek scowled at the memory of what must have been a terrifying time for him, discovering that she had vanished without a trace. Annora knew that they had much to discuss about all that had happened since then, but this was hardly the time whilst other were in listening distance. "I will not fail you again," he repeated before waving forward two knights. "Let me introduce you to Percival Ford and Manfred Crump. Both men can be trusted and have offered their services to ensure your safety."

Annora bowed her head. "Gentlemen. 'Tis kind of you to assist Merek, not that I cannot defend myself."

"Lady de Maris," both men said in unison giving her a nod from atop their horses.

Her tent was now loaded into the wagon with everything secured and they only waited for her command to follow the rest of Stephen's army. The cart began to move toward the road and she pointed in the direction they were to travel. "You may proceed us. We will follow directly."

Percival looked askance to Merek who nodded his head, and the men began to follow her wagon to the road. This left her and Merek mostly alone to have a brief conversation in relative privacy.

Annora pulled on her leather gloves that had been tucked into her waist. "Do you know where Stephen's army is headed next?" she asked.

"Nay. I do not think we shall be privy to such confidential information from now on."

"Why?"

One of Merek's brows rose. "You have to ask? I think you being captured by his enemy was enough to make Stephen leery of how much you might overhear. He fears you might have formed new allegiances and could somehow find a way to inform Empress Matilda of his plans in the future."

"I was hardly in the confidence of the Empress… who, as you know, had escaped days ago."

"But you were held by her supporters. And given your embrace of your captor before your exit from the keep, it may appear to Stephen—and to others—as though you are now on friendly terms with those that support the Empress, your enemy." Merek leaned an elbow on the pommel of his saddle while he stared directly upon her. "We have not had an opportunity to discuss what happened to you."

"What is there to discuss? I was captured and taken prisoner. Let it be enough that I was unharmed and treated with the utmost respect."

"I think there is plenty to discuss, Annora," Merek said reverting back to the familiar pattern of address she had become used to now that 'twas just the two of them. "I cannot believe that you were immune to the charms of Grancourt, given how familiar you appeared with him."

"We found a common accord in the short span of time we were in each other's company," she replied taking a brief glance toward the castle.

"Is that all?" he snarled with a frown.

She returned her attention to Merek to look him directly in his eyes. "We found a common ground. That is all. Nothing else happened between us," she fumed. 'Twas as though her captain wished to make what had occurred between her and Richard into something she should be ashamed of. Nothing could be farther from the truth.

"If you say so, Annora, but that was not how it appeared. At least, not to me. Your departure from the knight was one of two lovers saying farewell and not two people who met on a battlefield months ago when the city of Oxford fell into Stephen's hands," he muttered with an angry scowl upon his brow.

"Nothing happened between us that you need to be concerned about," Annora repeated. They had only shared a few stolen kisses, nothing more. And surely those mattered little now that her time with Richard was at an end. "Let the matter rest, Merek."

Merek took up his reins. "If you tell me you are the same as before you were captured, then so be it, but I think you speak a falsehood. I will, as you just ordered, let the matter rest. That is… for now. Let us catch up with the men who were willing to help guard you."

Merek flicked his reins and his horse moved forward leaving Annora a moment to herself.

Annora pondered Merek's words. She would *never* be the same as she used to be before she had been captured. She would be haunted by a pair of blue eyes for months if not years to come.

Annora tried to avoid looking in the direction of the fortress that she had lived in the shadows of for the past several months. But 'twas unavoidable as she hoped she would catch one last glimpse of a man who had somehow entered her heart. 'Twas foolish to continue to think of him. She knew this with every breath she took. Yet the warrior who had captured her against her will had somehow cracked the surface of the guard she had placed around her for more years than she could count. Richard Grancourt would be hard for her to ever forget.

With one last look at the battlements above the keep, she pulled on Shadow's reins to follow the men. Annora's time here at Oxford was at an end.

CHAPTER THIRTEEN

Richard peered off into the distance to watch the last of Stephen's army leave the city of Oxford. He had hoped to come to the battlement wall earlier to see if he could catch a last glimpse of Annora but had been detained with other responsibilities to the people who would remain at the keep. He had many duties to fulfill before he, too, would leave the city but he indulged in this one whim to a lady who had unexpectedly crawled her way into his heart.

Could he dare call what was between him and Annora love? These emotions that overwhelmed him were new to him and perchance 'twas too soon to call the situation he now found himself in love. Infatuation, certainly. Desire, most definitely. But love? He shook his head in denial that the emotion that had evaded him for his entire life might even now have found him. Richard needed to get his head back to where it belonged and not lose himself in fanciful thoughts of a lady who might one day be his if they could only find a way to be together. He had no idea when he might even lay eyes on the woman again and could only pray 'twould not be on another battlefield.

He tore himself away from the edge of the wall with a grunt of annoyance knowing he should not have even bothered to come up here in the first place. 'Twas a waste of his time when he had more important things to take care of to ensure all was in place before he left and headed for Devizes. As he made his way down the turret stairs, Richard then stopped on the floor where his bedchamber was located. He came across Oswin who paced near Beatrix's door.

"Is my sister inside?" Richard asked wondering what was bothering his friend. With Beatrix, anything was possible.

"She is irate with me," Oswin said with a scowl.

Richard chuckled. "When is she not upset about some matter of late? What did you do to earn her displeasure this time?"

Oswin threw up his hands. "I only told her to slow down as she ate the meal that had been provided. I warned her if she ate too fast, she might lose it all again but she would not listen."

"Let me guess... she vomited in the great hall to be witnessed by all?"

"And yelled at me that I was to blame," Oswin said in annoyance.

Richard slapped his friend on the back. "Best get used to such turmoil in your life if you plan to have any sort of a relationship with my sister."

One of Oswin's brows lifted. "You would not object to the idea of me courting her?"

Richard paused to contemplate the man before him. He could not foresee why Oswin would not make his sister a fitting husband but still... could she handle what the knight's duties might entail?

"I can see that you care for Beatrix, and I do not suppose there is any reason why I should object to a union between you. You are a man of honor and one of the Empress's champions. My only concern is that I cannot see Beatrix finding happiness as a camp wife, following you from one place to the next."

Oswin gave a sigh of what Richard assumed was relief. "If we were to wed, I would ask the Empress to release me from my service so I might return home."

"Then mayhap all will work out for the best. I trust you with my sister's life, Oswin. Do not disappoint me," Richard warned taking hold of Oswin's shoulder.

"I will always protect her with *my* life," Oswin declared placing one fist over his heart.

Another chuckle left Richard's lips. "Let us pray the situation does not come to such a drastic conclusion—but, as I have said, knowing Beatrix, anything is possible. I wish you luck with her. If anyone can handle her, 'twould be you."

"Then mayhap you can get her to open her bedchamber door to me so we might have speech together."

"Now, *that*, I will leave to you. Having chosen to pledge yourself to her, 'tis now your duty far more than mine to manage her mood. But you had best make haste. I wish to leave for Devizes within the next hour. Beatrix had better be packing her belongings if she wishes them to accompany her."

"And the other ladies in waiting, too?" Oswin asked.

"Aye. I was just about to ask a servant to help them prepare for their departure. The Empress will want her ladies with her at the soonest opportunity." Richard gave Oswin a sly grin before he pounded on Beatrix's door having changed his mind about helping his friend. "Beatrix! Open up."

The door immediately swung open. "Richard, I—" She began frowning when she saw Oswin standing next to her brother.

"If you wish to take anything with you, sister, you best get to packing. Oswin will help you with your trunk," Richard said giving Beatrix a short bow.

Oswin gave Richard a glance. "May I?"

Richard waved his hand toward his sister. "By all means."

Beatrix stomped her foot. "If you think I will allow that man—"

Her words were quickly cut off when Oswin took her into his arms and began to thoroughly kiss her. Richard could not watch the display any longer and he made his way to his bedchamber. When he opened the door, he came to a complete halt.

He had the foolish fancy that if he closed his eyes, Annora might appear before him, for her presence lingered in the room like a ghost. The autumn-colored dress she wore that first night she came down to the hall was neatly folded and laying at the foot of the bed. He lifted the fabric to his nose and could still smell the slightest hint of the floral scent from the bath she had taken. Their time together had been but days and yet the memories flitted through his head as if they had shared a lifetime. Her memory, it seemed, would haunt his every waking hour from now on.

So, this is what it was like to actually fall in love, he mused and for the first time in his life he felt completely alone. Without Annora, an essential piece of him would remain missing until they could one day be reunited. He cursed knowing such a happening might take years. He could only ponder if the lady might wait for him. He knew that he would wait for *her*. She had somehow etched herself into his heart as if she had written her name upon it and now, he had no idea how he might go on with his life without her, even knowing his duties to the Empress would most likely only take him further away from Annora de Maris.

There was no sense in denying the inevitable. Love had somehow found him in the midst of war and his life had become dimmer the moment Annora left the great hall. But he would somehow remain hopeful. With such a thought, Richard renewed his vow that he would find Annora again no matter how long it took or what it might cost him.

CHAPTER FOURTEEN

THE NIGHT WAS brisk, and camp had at last quieted down. Annora held her hands out to the fire wondering if its warmth might seep into her heart. Once more her guard was up—as it should have been all along, for what had her days with Richard really gotten her but more heartache? She had known him but days and even those had been spent mostly arguing between them. How could that first kiss change everything? Apparently, she was not made of very stern stuff if Richard's touch could so easily turn her into a moon-eyed bit of fluff.

She sniffed and ran her sleeve over her eyes. *God's blood!* She would never survive whatever life would bring her if she continued to torment herself by thinking about what might have been if she could have stayed with Richard Grancourt. 'Twas best to forget him. And yet, as a heavy sigh of sorrow left her, she knew 'twould not be that easy.

"You will do yourself no good to brood over the matter, Annora," Merek said taking a seat next to her on the log she sat upon.

"I have no idea what you are talking about," she said quietly.

"How many years have I watched over you, my lady? You do not think I am aware when something… or someone… is troubling you?"

She turned to look at the knight who indeed knew her well. There was no point in lying to the man. "Something has… changed in me."

He gave a grunt of annoyance. "Something or someone?"

She shrugged. "Mayhap a little of both," she said as she recalled her feelings and her memories for a man she barely knew.

He tossed another log onto the fire and Annora watched the sparks disappear into the night sky. "Let me guess... this *change* had something to do with Richard Grancourt."

Annora picked up a large stick and began poking the limb further into the fire. "Aye."

"He did not harm you, or so you said. Do you recant those words now?" Merek asked watching her closely.

"Nay. He did not harm me in any way. He treated me with respect, even as we argued for several days before he... well... let us say we came to friendly terms. 'Twas better to be amicable than to constantly spar with the man."

"*Amicable*? From the looks between the two of you that I saw clear across the hall, I would say you became more than just being on *friendly terms*."

"He kissed me," she blurted out and waited for Merek's temper to erupt. But he only waited for her to continue. "Nothing more."

"And this is the change you spoke of?" he finally asked.

"Aye. I suppose it is. I have not been the same ever since nor can I get my mind off the man," she replied whilst she continued to poke at the flames in front of her. 'Twas a meaningless distraction from the conversation she was having with a man who was acting like a protective older brother.

"Hate and love... there is a fine line between the two emotions that can wreck mayhem with a person's mind," Merek mumbled.

A short laugh left her. "How funny... Richard basically said the same thing."

Merek harrumphed as though saying something almost identical to Richard was unpleasant to him. "I cannot discount his words, but I do remain concerned your head is not where it belongs, Annora."

She frowned, well aware that there was truth to his words. "I know. But I am positive I shall return to normal once we reach our destination, wherever that may be."

"'Tis mayhap best that you forget Grancourt. A man like that has but one thing on his mind and that is his duty to his Empress. He will not leave her side, much like yours must remain with King Stephen."

"Why cannot life be different, Merek? Why must I follow a king whom I hold no respect for?" she grumbled finally tossing the stick into the flames.

"You know that answer better than anyone, Annora. You align yourself with Stephen for the sake of your son and for the opportunity to once more claim your home when this is all over," Merek answered giving her a weak smile.

"Aye… my son and home. We are so close to the outskirts of Meregate, I swear I can taste the ocean mist on my lips. How I wish I could learn that Leif is well, and no harm has befallen him," Annora proclaimed hiding her face in her hands.

"And that is what you need to hold at the forefront of your mind, my lady. Leif and your home. All else will only cloud your judgement in the months to come."

She turned her head so her gaze could fall upon the man sitting next to her. "Perchance you are right, Merek. Thank you for reminding me of my responsibilities and why I must needs remain faithful to Stephen."

A chuckle left him. "You *must* be tired if you agree with me so readily."

"Clearly I am not of sound mind," she teased.

"Then let us take our rest. The morn will be upon us before we know it," he declared as he stood. He left her side but briefly, returning moments later holding two bedrolls that he immediately began laying out by the fire. "Sleep well, Annora."

"And you, my friend," she murmured.

She watched as Merek settled himself for the night before she too went to lay beneath the covers. And as she drifted off to take her ease for what remained of the eve, she was haunted in her dreams by a man with black hair and startling blue eyes. And in her slumber, he whispered words of love and what could be if only she would return to his side.

CHAPTER FIFTEEN

RICHARD, ALONG WITH those who had ridden with him from Oxford, entered the great hall of Devizes Castle amidst the sound of applause from those in attendance. Empress Matilda sat on a raised dais and beckoned him toward her with a wave of her hand. As he made his way forward, he nodded to Reynard and Elysande Norwood. Standing next to them were Blake Kennarde and Kingsley Goodee. 'Twas pleasing to all be reunited again, and Richard was gladdened to see that everyone who left with the Empress that chilly night appeared well. He dropped to one knee when he approached the Empress, as did those behind him.

"Welcome back, Lord Grancourt," the Empress declared as she clapped her hands. "Welcome back to you all, especially my ladies in waiting. How I have missed your company."

"I am your most humble servant, my Empress," Richard said after he was bid to rise. The Empress held out her hand and Richard stepped forward to kiss the ring set on her finger.

"I see that you have all fared well since I last set eyes upon you. Tell me, how did Stephen take the news that I had escaped his clutches yet again?" the Empress said with a sly grin of satisfaction.

"Although I was not taken into his confidence, he appeared as disappointed as you could imagine, Empress," Richard answered.

"And he accepted Oxford's surrender as we anticipated?"

"Aye, and without over taxing us with his demands. In fact, he readily gave the place up once he knew you were no longer within. I expected him to have been announced at the gates far earlier than the messenger appeared, however. That, too, played into our plans by allowing you the necessary time to reach Devizes. Nothing untoward happened along the way?" Richard asked once he delivered all the information to impart to the Empress.

"Other than the blinding cold you mean?" Empress Matilda inquired.

"Aye. Besides the weather. We already knew that would become a challenge."

The Empress nodded. "Nay. Other than the frigid cold, we managed well enough. But I have other news to impart. My brother Earl Robert is here at Devizes. He was on the way to Oxford to attack Stephen's men and secure my release, but when he learned of my escape, he diverted his plans and made haste to reach us here. He has brought my oldest son Henry with him."

Richard widened his eyes. Henry would be England's future king if all went according to the plans of the Empress. "You must have been overjoyed to be reunited with your son... and your brother, of course."

"Aye. I am most pleased. But tell me what happened to the woman whom you took prisoner the night of my escape. I do not see her with your party, which leads me to think she did not journey here with you. Or did you leave her in my dungeon?" The Empress took hold of a golden chalice and took a drink whilst waiting for Richard's reply.

"The woman's return to Stephen was the only stipulation he made to Oxford's surrender," Richard answered as he envisioned the last moment he saw the lady.

One of the Empress's brows rose in disbelief. "She must be highly important to him and his cause," she said, looking thoughtful.

"She serves that cause only because he holds her son and home in ransom to her obedience. I will fill you in on the particulars of Lady de Maris's predicament when we are allowed more privacy."

"De Maris? As in the lady from Meregate?" the Empress inquired.

"Aye. One and the same."

The Empress shuddered. "I am aware of what happened to the lady's husband. Beheading... such a nasty way to get one's point across. 'Tis suitable only for those who commit treason. If I recall, Lord Leofric died whilst proclaiming his loyalty to me—the words still hanging on his lips with his last breath."

Now it was Richard's turn to be surprised by the Empress's words. Annora had never gotten so far as to tell how her husband had perished, only that the deed occurred during a siege of the castle. "I believe the lady feels the same anger over the cruel death of her husband, my Empress."

"I understand she can wield a sword with efficiency. Much like Wymar and Theobald's wives. Mayhap she would be willing to help my cause if we could free her son from Stephen's grasp. I can never have enough knights loyal to my cause," Empress Matilda mused aloud.

Richard made every attempt to hide the pleasure he felt at the Empress's words. This was exactly what he had been praying might happen in order for Annora to be free. Before he could reply, the Empress continued with a wave of her hand.

"We shall talk later, you and I, after you have rested from your journey." The Empress rose whilst her court bowed and curtseyed until she left the room. Her ladies followed her including Elysande. Conversations erupted whilst Reynard, Blake, and Kingsley came to Richard.

Richard grabbed Reynard in a fierce embrace. "I am glad to see you, brother," he said affectionately to the younger man who he considered to be as much a sibling of his as was Beatrix.

"I thought you'd never arrive... at least before Elysande and I left for Blackmore."

Richard gaze fell to the younger man. "Clearly, you all made it without any further problems."

Blake chuckled, before thumping Richard upon the back. "Aye! The ice held, praise be to God."

Kingsley shivered. "I swear I can still hear the river cracking whilst I slumber. Most unpleasant."

Oswin gave the man a shove. "At least you were not left behind to starve to death."

Blake's brow rose. "I see the fair Beatrix is not far from your side. Did you finally win the lady over?"

Oswin shrugged. "We still have much to discuss."

Kingsley gave Oswin a playful shove. "I am certain you have a better agenda than just talking the fair lady to death."

Richard stepped forward. "This is my sister you are discussing. Have a care for her name."

Kingsley threw up his hands in a motion of surrender. "I meant no disrespect toward your sister.

A brief smirk flitted across Richard's face. "Beatrix is the least of my worries."

Blake's eyes went wide. "Then you *have* given Oswin your blessing for a match between them?"

"Aye, I have if she will have him, that is," Richard answered, and the men began to congratulate Oswin as if he had already wed the lady.

Reynard clapped his hands in glee. "Well, I for one can vouch for the pleasantness of wedded bliss. Now we just need to find ladies for the rest of you who remain unattached."

Oswin gave Richard a wink and placed his hand on Richard's shoulder. "This one may have already found his match… that is, if he can find her again."

Reynard laughed. "Found and lost her so quickly, Richard? I would have thought you would fare better with a lady you favored."

Richard cursed beneath his breath. "I have no time to dally with a woman currently. I am more concerned as to where the Empress's campaign goes from this point forward."

Blake rolled his eyes. "That is our Richard. Always more concerned with the matter at hand than the delicate situation of a woman's heart."

"Nothing delicate about this lady," Oswin added with a grin. "Why, she is as fierce a warrior as Ceridwen and Ingrid."

Kingsley let out a whistle. "That good? Then Richard has indeed met his match. If only we could be as lucky."

Richard motioned for the men to follow as he began to leave the hall. "Lady de Maris has her own problems she must come to terms with. If the Empress will allow me a company of knights, we may be able to eventually free her son and liberate her estate from the usurper's men who now control it."

Reynard cursed. "If Stephen has a large number of troops encamped at her home, you may find that you need an entire army if you plan to go against them. Besides, I highly doubt you'll be given enough forces to lay siege to the place."

Richard mumbled another curse. Reynard's words hit far closer to the truth than Richard would like to admit. He had no idea how many men were holding Annora's home in Stephen's name. If there were only a small enough contingent, laying siege to the castle might be possible. Of course, even if it could be captured, keeping it in the Empress's name might be an entirely different matter once Stephen learned it had fallen to his enemy.

Richard ran his hand over the back of his neck in frustration at what the future might hold. "Let us discuss our next moves or objectives in my bedchamber. A closed door without the curiosity of those at court will be welcomed."

The men followed Richard up to his room where they were able to speak freely about simpler times and what they could foresee for their future. But Richard's mind drifted to a lady with tawny hair and green eyes, and he could only ponder when, or if, he might see her again. Until then, his duties were to the Empress and wherever she might go next.

CHAPTER SIXTEEN

ANNORA PULLED ON Shadow's reins and briefly closed her eyes. The saltiness of the ocean breeze was at last upon her lips. The faint sound of the distant waves crashing into the shore gave her a calming sense of peace. She opened her eyes to stare ahead. 'Twas the castle now within her eyesight that caused her breath to hitch. *Home!* Meregate Castle rose tall on the motte and bailey bluff, the keep towering six stories high over the battlement walls. 'Twas a sight that had been absent from her eyes for well over a year and she did everything within her power not to rush forward knowing her son was within these very walls. He was so close!

"We cannot tarry long," Merek reminded her quietly.

"That Stephen allowed me this one concession is enough. At least for now…"

"Then let us proceed so you might see your son," Merek answered as he flicked the reins of his horse.

Annora gave Shadow's neck a pat before she pressed her knee into the horse's side to urge him forward. Brief images rose to the forefront of her mind as she at last drew near. She tried to calm her racing nerves by taking in deep gulps of air. But no matter how she might attempt to keep herself in check when they began to cross the drawbridge, she could in no way forget the memory of the terrible day when the castle had fallen into Stephen's hands. The memory of those who had lost their heads would always stay with her.

'Twas difficult to forget how they had looked when they had been placed upon pikes outside her very gates. Those same knights who had been faithful to her household and had fought with valor to protect Meregate's people, defeated and vilely disgraced. She had trained with them. Celebrated their marriages and the birth of their children. Her husband had been one of those knights and the ghastly sight when she had left Meregate unto a year ago still haunted her every hour, when she slept and when she was awake. 'Twas not a vision that could easily be forgotten.

She shook her head to clear her memories as they were hailed from above the barbican gatehouse. The portcullis lifted so they could enter. The dozen knights she could see standing guard above were unknown to her and she and Merek shared a silent look between them. That the gate was kept closed in the middle of the day told her much. Those who controlled her home until Stephen deemed her worthy enough to return would not take the chance of another invasion. With Stephen's men on their guard and putting every precaution in place, Annora would need an entire army to see Meregate free from Stephen's rule and clearly that was not a possibility under her current circumstances.

Annora rode her horse forward as they had entered the outer bailey. She took in the scene before her and witnessed large numbers of Stephen's men who were training to remain fit in the open area where she herself had spent many an hour. There were far more here than she had expected. That chances of taking back the castle narrowed even further, and Annora shook off any thoughts of regaining control without a large force behind her.

Leaving the area finally brought her into the inner bailey. Whilst she came closer to the keep, she took a closer look at the condition of her home. Apparently, whoever was overseeing Meregate had no notion to repair the damage to the buildings from Stephen's initial attack, for she noted that they continued to be falling around her. The people appeared half starved and weary, though when she jumped down from the saddle, several who were familiar to her began to bow and give her the respect they felt they still owed her. Their loyalty filled her heart with a brief moment of joy.

More knights unfamiliar to her came rushing forward to surround her whilst two others went to stand guard at the keep door. Whoever was the steward here clearly expected another battle to incur. They must be weak if they thought Annora and her captain could overtake Meregate with just the two of them. The fools.

One weeping woman came rushing from the stone structure of the keep and dropped to her knees at Annora's feet. "Lady de Maris… you are home! We have prayed daily for your safety."

Annora took hold of the woman's hands helping her to stand. "Edme… thank goodness you are safe," she proclaimed before she embraced the woman who had long attended her. "But there is no need to stand on ceremony for my benefit. I am but passing by and was given leave to see my son."

"There have been many changes since you were forced to leave your home, milady," Edme confessed softly, "and not for the better."

Annora took the woman's arm as she began to walk toward the steps of the keep. "'Tis clear to me that my people are not being taken care of in my absence. Are they not feeding you?"

The woman turned worried eyes downward. "I had best not complain, milady. Others are far worse off than I."

"Who has been running the place? I will take the matter up with him," Annora fumed, hating that she would clearly need to beg someone's favor to see that her people were properly fed. Fear flashed across Edme's visage and Annora patted her arm. "Never mind. I shall not put you in a position where you might bear the brunt of my actions."

"You will not be… pleased, milady."

"Nay, that is certain. But first things first. Find Leif and bring him to me in the great hall," Annora asked watching the woman leave.

Not even in my own home and already I will need to plead for my people. What condition is my son in if the inhabitants of Meregate are half starved? she thought before calling over her shoulder. "Merek! Come with me."

Her ever-faithful knight fell into step but not before he voiced his thoughts aloud. "I like not what is going on here. You had best prepare yourself for the worst."

"Aye. Whoever is holding Meregate in Stephen's name does not appear to care much for those who keep the place running efficiently. Clearly, he is only concerned for his own needs."

They came to the entrance to the keep and the two guards continued to bar their way inside.

"Stand aside and allow Lady de Maris entrance," Merek ordered placing his hand on the hilt of his sword.

"You have been expected," one of the guardsmen answered looking her up and down as if assessing her worth. "And you are late."

Annora raised one of her brows. "I am on time according to my own schedule. Now, let me pass."

The other knight pounded on the door and Annora could detect the sound of the iron bar being raised on the other side. When the portal finally opened, she stepped forward until she was finally standing in the entryway to her home. Yet nothing endearing about the foyer gave her comfort. Gone were her vases and gold trinkets that once stood on a table near the turret. In fact, the wooden table had been reduced to rubble and no one had bothered to clean up the mess. *Breathe...* she told herself before her feet took her toward the right where the great hall was located. She came to a sudden halt.

Her hall had not fared any better than the entranceway. What remained of her tapestries hung in shreds as they had been slashed to pieces. Remains of the tables and chairs were in piles, but a glance alone was enough to tell her there would not be much to salvage. In fact, the only thing they could be used for would be fuel for the fires to warm the place. But what shocked her the most was the man sitting in her husband's chair. The very man who had killed her husband. Clifton Tashe… her sworn enemy.

"Ah… the lady finally returns home. Step forward, Lady de Maris," Clifton ordered, waving his hand for her to obey his command.

Merek bent to speak directly in her ear. "Do not do anything rash, Annora. Remember you are here to see your son. You cannot do anything more than that if you lose your temper."

"But he is—"

"He is the man you will one day have the pleasure of killing for his past sins but for now he is the one person who stands in the way of you being permitted to seeing your son," Merek reminded her.

Annora knew Merek was right but everything inside her refused to back down, reminding her how badly she wanted to punish this man for all he had done. He was a traitor to the Empress, but he was also a neighboring landholder who had been after Meregate's prime port location for as long as Annora could remember.

Meregate had been her holding prior to her marriage. The management had been bestowed upon Leofric once they had wed, although he had allowed her to voice her input on her home's interests. She knew every nook and cranny of this estate and she would be damned if she would allow Tashe to tarnish the memories she held dear.

Annora began to advance, and the closer she drew to Clifton Tashe, the more her anger grew to the point where she longed to thrust her sword into his gut. It was almost strong enough to overpower her—*almost*. Even in the height of her anger, she knew that if she wished to see Leif, then she needed to dig deep to keep her temper in check. Still… he sat at his chair with a banquet of food within his reach that could feed half the people at Meregate for the next several days, and the sight filled her with disgust.

His protruding belly told her much… the people might be starving but he certainly was not. His general appearance was abhorrent, and she could only wonder when the last time was that this man had decided to bathe. His long brown hair hung in oily strands. His tunic was covered in grease where he had wiped his fingers over the fabric. If she looked hard enough, she imagined she'd be able to see particles of his meal within his unkept beard.

But 'twas the unsightly grin that he bestowed upon her that had her reaching for the hilt of her blade. His eyes lit up with what she perceived as desire. Now, in a mere matter of seconds, Annora again wanted nothing more than to run this scoundrel through.

"Easy, Annora," Merek whispered from behind her. She took a deep breath and then took her fingertips from the blade at her side.

When she at last stood before her enemy, she did not bother to pay him any sort of formal courtesy of respect. He had not earned such an honor so, in her mind's eye, what was the point of pretending by bestowing something upon him that he did not deserve? But neither did she attack him. She would be restrained—for her son's sake.

"Tashe…" she managed to voice between clenched teeth. "I see you are up to your usual… appetites."

"Annora…" he said licking his lips before reaching for a chalice and downing its contents. "Stubborn as always, I see. Do you not think it would benefit you to grovel at my feet?

A snort left her. "'Twill be a cold day in hell before such a miracle as that occurs. I am here—with King Stephen's blessing—to see my son. Nothing more."

Clifton leaned forward. "You should still pay me the respect due me as I am now lord here." He sat back in his chair with the confidence of one who relished being in charge. Another pleased smile slid across his lips.

'Twas Annora's turn to now be amused and a sarcastic laugh left her mouth. "Is that so?" she said taking a step forward. "Something must have changed in the last hour since I spoke to our King, for he informed me that once my service to him has finished I will return to my home to govern it."

A crack in Clifton's gloating expression briefly appeared before he placed a mask of indifference upon his face. "Aye… so I have been informed. 'Tis the reason why I have asked for you and I to wed. I but await the King's decision on the matter."

Annora choked back a gasp of shock. Married? To this foul scum? She would rather be forced into a nunnery than be wed to the man who killed her husband. Clifton began laughing, causing Annora to once again struggle to choke back the words she wished to throw in his face. Her patience was fading piece by piece the longer she had to stand in his presence.

Clifton clapped his hands in glee. "Finally! I have at last said something that has forced you to take my words seriously. I shall look forward to the day when we have married and you will have no choice but to obey my every command."

She would not let this man get the better of her. She forced herself to regain her calm. She folded her arms over her chest and finally found her voice. "As I said… 'twill be a cold day in hell. But if such thoughts make you feel better for the sins you have committed, you may wallow away in them. I have no time to continue holding speech with someone who shall one day be a servant to the devil."

Clifton pointed at her, his face turning red in outrage. There was a small flit of satisfaction that upturned the corner of her mouth at the thought that she would not bow down and concede to what he thought awaited her fate. "You *will* be my wife!"

Annora lifted her brow and gave a crooked smile. "Nay. I will not." She was about to say more when the sound of running feet caused her heart to soar.

"Mama!" her son called.

Leif came running into the hall. 'Twas hard to imagine that her son would soon be eight summers as she watched him lessen the distance between them. None who looked at him could doubt this was her son with his tawny-colored hair and matching green eyes that sparkled in delight that his mother had returned home. She knelt down and opened her arms wide until he threw himself into her embrace. Tears of joy raced down her cheeks and she shed them freely before she looked up into Merek's face to see him smiling. He held out his hand to her.

"Come, my lady, and let us find a quiet space for you to speak with your son."

Annora took her captain's hand and reached for Leif's with the other. Her time with her son was precious and she would not waste a moment of it wallowing away in self-pity on what the future might hold for her here at Meregate Castle.

CHAPTER SEVENTEEN

RICHARD APPROACHED THE door to the Empress's solar with a trace of trepidation in his heart. He had no idea why he had been summoned for a private conversation with the Empress but whatever was about to happen he had the notion that it could not be good news. Call it intuition or just some nagging feeling deep inside him, but all his nerves felt on edge…though he would confess that part of his turmoil stemmed from worrying about the fate of a certain lady he could not get off his mind. Between Annora's plight and Beatrix hounding him about how she wished to return home, he could only pray that another catastrophe did not await him inside.

The guard standing at the entrance to the room immediately opened the portal when Richard approached, giving evidence that he was expected. He crossed the solar and took a knee before the lady.

"Take yourself from the floor, Grancourt, and instead take a chair beside me," the Empress ordered causing Richard's eyes to go wide at the unexpected privilege.

"You are too gracious, my Empress," Richard replied before sitting in the chair she'd offered him. He stole a glance at the Empress's brother, Earl Robert, sitting in the opposite seat. Richard gave the man a slight nod which Robert returned.

"You are most likely wondering why I have called you here, Richard," Empress Matilda began, startling him again. She was not in the habit of calling her knights by their given names.

"I am yours to command, Empress," Richard answered politely.

Before she continued, she turned her attention to a nearby servant. "Provide us wine and then you may leave us."

The pouring of wine splashing into chalices was the only sound in the room with the exception of the crackling fire in the hearth. Richard was offered a goblet. He took a sip of his drink but did not drink heavily. Whatever was coming, if the Empress thought he needed to be softened up to it with alcohol then he would, in contrast, be wise to keep a clear head.

"Your service to me has been invaluable to my cause," Empress Matilda remarked as she, too, took a sip from her cup. She set her golden chalice down and gave a weary sigh. "Robert and I have had a heavy discussion for the past several days on where my campaign for the throne is headed."

Richard also put down his goblet. "I assumed now that you had made your escape from Oxford that you would resume your efforts to seize lands currently controlled by the usurper."

Robert shook his head. "Unfortunately, my sister and I have decided that if we were to continue such a course, this would only cause this war to continue on for years to come, plunging the country into further mayhem."

Richard nodded his understanding. As strongly as he supported the Empress's cause, he knew in his heart that to continue the fight would be to prolong the suffering of countless people. The citizens of England were already close to starving from the years the war had lingered with neither side gaining much ground. Matilda was no closer to sitting upon the throne now than when her efforts started years ago.

Matilda raised her hand to her brow. "We have come to the conclusion that I may never sit on England's throne."

Richard came forward in his chair. "But Empress—"

"Hear her out, Grancourt," Robert replied.

"Of course, my lord," Richard said waiting for Empress Matilda to continue.

Matilda leaned her head back on her chair before she turned her eyes to Richard. "*I may not sit on the throne, but my son will do so when the time comes.*"

"Henry..." Richard whispered.

"Aye," the Empress proclaimed. "He is young still at only nine summers, but I am placing him in my brother's care to prepare him for the position he will hold. Robert is the best solution to foster the child and teach him all he must needs know. When he gets older, I will once again take over his tutoring so he will one day become a great ruler."

"And what does this all have to do with me, my Empress?" Richard asked, feeling at a loss as to where his life might now take him.

"You will help my cause by following my brother. He recently lost his captain of guard to an illness after their journey home from Normandy. You, Richard, will take his place," Empress Matilda declared.

Richard's eyes went wide. The Empress was sending him away? Did that mean he had lost her favor? "What have I done to displease you, Empress, that you would send me away from guarding you?"

Robert leaned forward. "You have done nothing, Grancourt, other than to serve your Empress well. Think of this as an advancement. Not only will you become captain of my men, but you will be protecting the child who is the future King of England."

"I am honored for the privilege but who will see to your safety, Empress?" Richard asked.

Empress Matilda reached for her chalice again. "I have enough knights here to guard me for the time being. And I may soon end up back in Normandy where I will be safe with my husband's army as guards. However, I give you leave to take Kennarde, Goodee, and Woodwarde with you. You might need the strength of their swords in the coming months given the battles Robert may be forced to fight on my behalf before this war can end."

Beatrix's face floated into his mind. He figured that now was a good a time as any to plead her cause. "My Empress... as to Oswin Woodwarde..."

The Empress's brow rose. "What of him? Has he offended you in some way? Do you wish to tell me that you no longer trust him?"

"Nothing of the sort, Empress."

"Then what is the issue with him traveling with you and my brother?"

Richard reached for his own goblet and took a drink before putting the cup back down. "He is in love with my sister. With your approval, I am asking permission for them to wed."

'Twas the Empress's turn to stare in wonder at Richard. "You approve of their union?"

"Aye, but only if they might be released from their service to you so that they might return to Oswin's home to live out their lives. Only then he would be a suitable husband to Beatrix," Richard answered hoping he was not speaking out of line or too soon. He had not spoken to Beatrix as yet about her feelings for Oswin and could only assume she cared for the man as much as he did for her.

"He has estates near your home at Lyndhurst, does he not?" Empress Matilda inquired, and Richard could almost read her thoughts. No doubt she was pleased at the prospect that another landholder in the west would be loyal to her cause.

"Aye. Oswin's home is at Ashurst to the northeast of my own land," Richard answered softly.

"That *is* convenient..." Empress Matilda nodded tapping her chin as she contemplated this new development. "I will speak to Lady Beatrix to ensure she is amicable to a union with Woodwarde. If she is in agreement, and so is the gentleman, then we shall have a wedding prior to your departure."

"You are too gracious, my Empress," Richard said with a slight bow.

"Their union would benefit my cause and makes sense," the Empress replied with a smile of satisfaction. "You and my brother can work out the arrangements for when you will travel and where you will head next. In the meantime, I give you leave to have speech with Woodwarde whilst I summon your sister to attend me."

Richard stood and gave the Empress a bow before he left the room. Once in the passageway, he turned back to stare at the woman he had served for many years. He wondered what her future held now that she was no longer seeking to gain the throne. He shook his head and went to find Oswin, hoping he was bringing his friend good news.

CHAPTER EIGHTEEN

Annora held her sleeping child in her lap wishing with all her might that she did not have to leave him. She had been lucky she had even been allowed this much time to spend with him but 'twas not fair that she must leave him so soon. She had known 'twould be hard to let go again once she had the boy in her arms. She just had not known that a piece of her heart would be ripped to shreds with their parting. Tears welled in her eyes at the injustice of it all, but she had little choice in the matter. She would need to leave Meregate within the hour.

Edme returned to the room that had once belonged to Annora and Leofric and waited by the door whilst Annora continued to rock her child. As with the rest of the castle, nothing of any value remained from when she had resided here. 'Twas as though Tashe had sold everything he hadn't destroyed just to put more food in his own belly. Or mayhap he had stored her valuables away until he could fetch a decent price for them to one day line his own coffers. In either case, she cared little. The items lost weren't important to her—not compared to her people, who were quite clearly starving to death. She would see what she could find in Meregate's kitchen so she might feed those who were in the most need.

"'Tis time, milady," Edme whispered stepping into the room.

"Leif, my love," Annora said softly in the lad's ear. "Wake up, dear boy."

Leif lifted his head and rubbed his sleepy eyes. "I was dreaming you could stay…" he said patting her cheek.

"If only I could," Annora said choking back a sob. "But we will be together again, soon. I promise."

Leif threw his arms around her neck. "I will miss you. 'Tis not the same here without you, Mama."

She stroked the boy's tawny hair that was the same shade as her own. "Promise me you will be good. Stay out of mischief and hide if trouble attempts to find you."

"I promise," he vowed with a tiny smile.

She kissed both his cheeks and gave him one last hug. "Off you go with Edme. I love you."

"Love you, too, Mama."

Her son waved farewell and Annora stood knowing she would need to hurry if she wanted to see the servants fed before she left. She was certain there must be enough food in her larder, and she would not allow Clifton to fatten his belly even more if she could do something about the situation. Given the banquet that had been laid out for his consumption upon her arrival, the kitchen must have survived in order to feed its current steward.

She reached the turret and was about to descend the curved stairs when she saw Merek coming up them, no doubt in search of her. He wore a frown, and she could only guess as to the reason.

He turned around and joined her, descending the stairs by her side. "What news have you learned?" she asked when she reached the ground floor. He moved toward the exit but stopped in his tracks when she turned right instead, into a passageway that would take her around the great hall to reach the kitchen area.

Merek cursed. "You were right about the remaining knights loyal to Meregate. They are in the dungeon. If you think Edme and the other servants appear in need of food, that is nothing compared to those men below."

"Damn Tashe to hell," Annora cursed taking hold of Merek's arm and leading him into an alcove so they could remain unseen. "We will get whatever we can from the kitchen to see them fed if this is even possible. I will not know the state of the larder until I see what remains for myself. On our return, we'll scour the cellars for even more if this, too, survived Tashe's destruction so the household staff and my son will not go to bed hungry tonight."

"What if we are caught?" Merek asked with a crooked grin that told her his argument was only for form's sake. He was not truly trying to stop her, merely make her consider the possible consequences.

"What more can they do to me? Besides, I am here by order of King Stephen. I highly doubt they would take us prisoner when 'tis known that we must report back to duty. They could not be that foolish," she huffed in annoyance.

A snort left the man beside her. "Clifton Tashe is and always will be a brazen arse."

"You have that aright but for now he is the least of my worries. Let Tashe be hungry for a change but tonight my people will have a feast!"

Feast... hopefully she would not have to retract those words.

As she entered the kitchen, she could see for herself that the evening meal was in the process of being prepared. Annora narrowed her eyes when she saw another banquet that would be served to one man, and perhaps to those most loyal to him. There could not be many who would fit that description, given what she, herself, knew of Tashe's reputation.

She came into the kitchen with her hands on her hips whilst her eyes roamed the room, spotting various foods she could easily carry down to her men in the dungeons. If possible, she would release them, but first she needed to make sure they had at the very least food and something to drink.

A large unknown man came out of a room that Annora knew served as a pantry. He carried a basket with fruits and vegetables but stopped in his tracks and growled in outrage when he realized that a woman was in his domain.

"Get out!" he ordered with a wave of his free hand. "You do not belong in here."

Merek took a menacing step forward with his hand on the hilt of his sword. "Watch your tongue. This is Lady Annora de Maris, and this is her household."

The man hefted a heavy cast iron skillet in the air. "Not anymore. This castle belongs to Lord Tashe."

Merek pulled out his blade and Annora watched the man gulp when the point was at his throat. "He is but a steward here until the lady's return. I suggest you give her the respect that is due her." Merek pulled back his sword once the man gave the briefest of nods, but her captain still held the weapon in the direction of the cook. The man rubbed at his neck.

"Milady," the cook pronounced begrudgingly, whilst other kitchen staff began to also bow toward Annora.

Annora gave them a brief nod of her head before she began inspecting the various pots that were positioned on a swinging iron rod over the fire. Taking hold of a rag from one of the tables, she lifted the lid to find a sizable stew ready for tasting. She thrust out her hand and a servant ran for a wooden spoon and handed it to her. She took a scoop of stew, sniffed the contents, and then blew air on the food to cool it before she lifted the spoon to her lips. She smiled in pleasure at the taste. This man might have the personality of a foul beast, but he could at least cook!

"Is all this for Tashe?" Annora asked before she held out her hand for the basket the cook held. She dumped out the vegetables and fruit onto the wooden table before she leveled her gaze on the man who had yet to answer. "Merek… your blade. I believe Cook will cooperate now that he knows I am the lady of the keep."

Merek at last lowered his sword and put the blade back in his scabbard. Cook let out a sigh of relief.

"Aye. 'Tis all for him, milady. He expects the best and we wish only to please him. The last of the kitchen staff did not fare well after they were found feeding themselves and others who were hungry." The man seemed sincere. She could not claim to be impressed with his callousness, caring only for his own safety when others were starving, but at least he was honest about it.

"I see. Well, I am here to make a few changes until my return. I expect my people to be fed including my son and those who answer to me. I will not have any of my people starve because of one man's greed and gluttony. Is this understood?" Annora asked leveling her eyes on the kitchen staff.

"Aye, milady. But what happens after you are gone?" Cook asked with a worried expression.

"Leave that to me. I will deal with Tashe before I leave and ensure that everyone will be safe. No harm will come to you from following my orders," Annora declared hoping she would be able to keep such a promise. She could only do her best to ensure that the threat she planned to leave with Tashe would hold him in check until her return.

She began issuing orders for food to be served to her people. The amount that was to be reserved to feed Tashe and his followers were cut more than in half. Her gaze traveled to the far corner of the room and the doorway that led down into the bowels of the castle. Her loyal men were down there being held prisoner and she was now more than ever determined to see that they were set at liberty.

"Merek," she called out, "let us see about freeing our comrades in arms."

Merek nodded and pulled his sword from his scabbard as he began leading the way down the stairs to the dungeon. The farther down into the depths they went, the cooler the air became and Annora could only wonder the fate of the men who had been held here for months. They had been faithful servants to her household and she swore she would see them free from their prison.

A guard that must be a follower to Tashe sat on a small stool at a wooden table. He quickly came to attention upon their arrival. He attempted at first to pull his sword from his scabbard, but he froze when he found Merek's blade at his throat.

"I would think very carefully before you make any further attempts to draw your blade, my friend," Merek warned pressing the tip of his blade against his skin. Close… but not enough to spill blood.

Annora stepped forward. "Give me the keys to the cells," she ordered holding out her hand.

The guard pointed behind her. "They are hanging on the wall, my lady," he declared whilst attempting not to gulp.

"Watch him carefully, Merek," she said reaching for the ring hanging on a peg.

"I do not think he is going anywhere, Lady de Maris," Merek replied with a smirk.

"De Maris?" the man questioned.

"Aye. The lady of the keep," Merek replied, "and she is here to free her men."

The men who had been locked up for months gradually seemed to realize that something was going on, stirring themselves from the stupor they had fallen into. Annora went to the first cell and began fumbling with the keys to see which one would unlock her knights. She barely recognized one who had been her husband's captain. He was filthy now, with a long beard that hid most of his face. His fingers went around the bars whilst his eyes—the only part of him that she recognized—went wide.

"Am I imagining you are here, my lady?" Sir Wolfe Haywoode asked in apparent disbelief.

"I am here, Wolfe, to free you and the rest of the men," Annora answered when the right key finally clicked into place, and she was able to swing the door open.

Wolfe immediately fell to his knees before her. "My lady."

"Please rise, Wolfe, if you are able, and help those who are in worse condition. You shall all eat well this day and return above to your quarters," Annora announced whilst the men gave a small cheer of gratitude. She went to the next several cells and performed the same service, freeing over two dozen of her men. She looked around, knowing several were still missing.

"Where are the rest?" she asked with a frown of displeasure.

Wolfe stepped forward. "The rest either did not make it through the initial conflict or succumbed to their injuries in the days that followed. One man was thrown into the pit but we have not heard him call out for some time."

"I swear I will fill that damn thing in upon my return," Annora swore as she went to the bars covering the hole in the floor. "Someone hand me a torch."

She again fumbled with the keys to see which one would open the lock, knowing the iron rods prevented anyone from falling down to the pit's depths. The pit was deep and there was no way for anyone to climb up the slippery walls to their freedom from such a prison. With the lock opened and torch in hand, she peered down into the pit. The stench made her want to retch but she held it together hoping against hope that her knight might have survived, despite all the odds against him. She called down to what appeared to be the form of a man hunched in a fetal position but there was no answer. She could only assume the worst. She was about to declare him dead, when a slight motion made her look down again. The man barely had enough energy to raise his hand but 'twas enough to know he yet lived.

"Merek, bring our newfound friend over. Since he was so instrumental in keeping an eye on our men, he can be the lucky one to retrieve the one he left in this God forsaken pit," Annora said as she located a length of rope that was kept nearby for just such an occasion.

Once the knight had been brought topside, Annora and her men all began to help each other up the long set of stairs. Most of them were as weak as newborn kittens and the effort to climb took what remained of their energy. As they reached the kitchen, she came to the conclusion that she would need to leave Merek behind in order to see that her knights were not returned to the dungeons. Knowing her friend and captain, he would not be pleased to be parted from her, but she could only hope he would obey her command, for the sake of keeping his comrades alive.

CHAPTER NINETEEN

RICHARD WAS AT last allowed entrance into Beatrix's bedchamber. Her light blue gown was stunning along with the jewels that hung from her neck, ears, and wrist. She certainly appeared as a happy bride-to-be and Richard was thrilled for his little sister who had found a man worthy of her.

Coming into the room, he reached for her hands and brought her fingertips to his lips. Seeing how radiant Beatrix appeared calmed his racing heart and silenced any lingering objections he had still been holding for her wedding. The Empress had informed Richard that Oswin and Beatrix would be allowed to leave her service after they wed, but until such information was official, Richard continued to be on edge. 'Twould not be the first time a monarch had gone back on their word.

"You are beautiful, sister," Richard sighed giving her a bright smile before he pulled her into his embrace.

"Do you think Oswin will agree?" she asked breathlessly.

"Aye... that is, if he knows what is good for him," Richard chuckled before cupping her face. "Tell me you are happy, and that you have no regrets."

"Oh, Richard... such a question," she answered with a wave of her hand. "Of course, I am happy. I am about to wed the man I love. Why would I not be happy?"

"I just wanted to make sure. If you have any doubts, there is still time to change your mind. You have not yet said your vows before the priest. We could cancel the ceremony entirely, if you say that that's what you want."

Beatrix's eyes went wide. "I will do no such thing. I love Oswin and will wed no other!"

"Then, I am indeed happy for you, Beatrix. All I ever wanted was for you to find the man who would make your heart soar," Richard replied.

She gave a light laugh. "You sound so romantic, Richard. 'Tis not at all what I would have expected from you, given your manner as of late."

"Just because I do not go around spouting flowery words to praise the beauty of the women at court, does not mean I do not have a soft spot for those I care about," he replied going to the window and opening the shutter to peer outside.

"Like Lady de Maris?" Beatrix asked and Richard could have sworn a part of his heart cracked wide open just hearing another saying her name.

Richard sighed and closed his eyes, allowing himself the indulgence of envisioning the lady and imagining what she might be doing right now. But after a moment, he let the image go, forcing himself to focus on the present once more. "We are on different paths."

"But your heart tells me otherwise," Beatrix said coming to his side and placing her hand on his arm. "You could go and find her, Richard."

He closed the shutter and patted his sister's hand. "'Tis not that simple. Besides, you know full well that I will be off to serve under Earl Robert soon. Only the good Lord above knows where such an excursion will take me."

"Mayhap eventually your journey will take you back to her side. I do not wish for you to be alone, brother, and she is the first woman in many a year that you have shown the smallest affection for. I would hate for you to lose such an opportunity to find a wife who may be perfect for you."

A smirk crept up at the corner of his mouth. "Look who suddenly sounds like the voice of reason. If I did not know better, I would swear you are the elder sibling."

Beatrix gave a small shrug of her shoulders. "I saw the two of you together at Oxford, Richard. Only a fool would have dismissed the signs that you cared for each other."

'Twas Richard's turn to shrug. "Why... we barely knew one another."

Beatrix wagged her finger at him. "Sometimes two hearts just know when they have found their other half. I have the notion you were meant to be together. Do not dismiss what you feel for the lady. Nor should you wait too long to claim her. If you delay overmuch, you may come to regret it."

I already do, he thought miserably but shook himself out of his sudden doldrums. "Wherever my fate might lie, 'tis not something that must needs be addressed today of all days. You, dearest sister, are about to wed one of my close friends. Shall we get you below to the chapel?" he asked holding out his arm.

"Aye," she answered placing her fingers lightly into the crook of his elbow.

The rest of the ceremony became a blur as he watched his sister and Oswin have their union blessed by Empress Matilda's priest. An accounting of what each brought to their marriage was recorded by a scribe and with the Empress's approval, their marriage document was signed and sealed.

The feast in the great hall to celebrate was quite grand, and Richard was indeed pleased for his sister. There could be no doubt in his mind that Beatrix was happy as the minstrels picked up their lutes and their music filled the hall. Beatrix and Oswin made their way to dance in each other's arms to the lively tune whilst others came to join in on the merriment. His sister's laughter filled the great hall causing Richard's heart to be filled with joy at her clear contentment, safely enveloped in the arms of the man she loved. 'Twas all he ever wanted for her.

Aye. She had made a good match. Oswin would be a strong enough partner to put up with Beatrix's antics when she became too stubborn for her own good. Richard knew such a trait would not easily be diminished for she had a strong personality. Oswin was just the man to tame the woman while not crushing her spirits.

Hopefully their lives would not be disrupted with any battles at their gates and they could live out the rest of their lives in peace. If only Richard could be so lucky. He had not time to allow love into his world. For that reason, 'twas best that he forget all about his feelings for Annora. He had the notion that he would be lifting his blade soon as he continued to defend his life all in the name of Empress Matilda.

CHAPTER TWENTY

Annora sat in her husband's chair in the great hall waiting for Clifton Tashe to answer her summons. The man had taken an afternoon nap. Most likely, he had need of it to nurse an aching head after too much drink. Her cellars would need to be replenished by the time she was able to return.

She did not have long to wait since she began to hear the scoundrel before she ever saw him. His angry voice echoed in the turret as he issued orders for wine to be brought to him. When he gained the entrance to the hall, his boots came to a skidding halt when he saw her sitting in her rightful place. Annora had the satisfaction of watching his mouth open and close several times before he snapped his lips shut and proceeded to come before her.

"You have no right—"

"I have every right," Annora hissed leaning forward in her chair. "You are but a temporary replacement here in my absence. *You* are not lord of Meregate nor will you ever be."

"King Stephen will learn of your insolence," Clifton warned pointing a finger at her. "He will receive a *full* account."

"Aye! He will get a fine accounting indeed, wherein he will learn of the gluttony of the fool he left here in my place! Have no doubt I will report to him everything that I have witnessed here. I have the notion that once my report is delivered, you will not be left as steward afterward for much longer," Annora declared with a satisfied smirk.

A sarcastic laugh left his lips. "The King is too busy trying to claim other estates than to bother with the way that this one is managed. I will return to doing what I please the moment you leave these gates," he said with a sly smile.

"We shall see about that, Tashe. In the meantime, if you have not already learned of the changes I have made, let me inform you of them. Personally, I am surprised you are even awake since you seem to spend many an hour drinking my wine cellars dry. But I have righted the wrong you have done here, Tashe. I have rescued my men from the dungeons and have seen that my people will no longer starve. Change any of that in my absence, and I will see that King Stephen deals with you accordingly," she warned.

"You do not have the King's confidence," he attempted whilst his smile faded from his lips.

"That I am here should have told you much. Now I must needs return to His Majesty so I can inform him that the steward he left until my return is not only a wastrel but is incompetent when it comes to watching over anything of import."

Annora rose from her chair and went to stand in front of the man whom she swore would one day pay for all he had done. "Do not attempt to starve my people again nor return my knights to the dungeons. If I hear you have done so, you will not only answer to me but also the King."

She swept past him in the hopes some of her words would penetrate his thick skull. She could only pray that her people would be safe from further harm. In truth her threats were only as good as the fear she instilled in Tashe.

As she left the keep and entered the courtyard, she saw that her son was waiting for her. Annora went to him and gave him a fierce hug, holding Leif to her as if this would be the last time she would see her son. A sob escaped her knowing her fears could come true. She could not foresee her future or what might come to pass other than she knew her life would be in danger with each battle she was forced to participate in.

The boy began to squirm in her arms and she had the notion that such coddling and shows of affection would not be tolerated in the future. Her son was growing up too fast and their relationship would take on another form as he grew to manhood.

"Mama... God speed to you," he whispered before he pulled himself out of her arms and stood there with arms crossed over his chest. He appeared so much like his father 'twas as though Leofric was reincarnated into their son.

She looked up at Leif and rose from the ground. "Behave and listen to Merek. He will keep you safe."

A sound much like snort left the boy. "I do not need anyone to keep me safe," he declared pulling out a small blade hidden in his boot. "I can do so myself and have learned these many months how to hide when trouble comes my way."

Annora was unsure whether to feel amusement at his bravado or horror that her own flesh and blood had to conceal a weapon on his young form in order to feel safe. He was becoming a man right before her very eyes and only God above knew when she would see him again.

"Humor me, Leif," she began and ruffled his hair only to hear the lad gasp in dismay when the sound of youthful laughter erupted by a group of boys nearby.

"Do not embarrass me, Mama," he interjected.

"Very well but please do as I say and listen to Merek. Think of him as an uncle," Annora said whilst her gaze traveled to the man holding the reins of Shadow.

"I will. Fare thee well, Mama," Leif said and began to leave her side. Looking over his shoulder, Annora's breath hitched when he ran back to hug her about her waist.

Annora smoothed back his hair and when he raised his face to stare upon her, she saw the glimmer of tears in his eyes. She wiped them away when they fell to his cheeks. "I love you, son."

"I love you, too, Mama."

She watched him finally run off to join the other boys. Whatever her son's future may hold, at least he had boys his own age who appeared to accept him as one of their own. But children belonging to her servants could in no way teach Leif all he must needs know as a son of nobility. She gave a heavy sigh knowing there was nothing more she could do for the lad for now. But soon... soon she would return and reclaim all that had been taken from her!

The sound of horses caused Annora to turn her attention toward her gate. She should not have been surprised when she saw Percival and Manfred—the guards that Stephen had assigned to her—come into the bailey leading a small group of knights. She supposed they had come at the suggestion of Stephen to lead her back to his army and wherever her life may now take her. Her time here at Meregate was at an end.

She made her way to her horse, preparing herself to hear whatever Merek was holding back. From his frown, she knew he would voice his objections to being left behind. He did not prove her wrong once he spoke.

"I do not like this," he grumbled whilst Annora stroked Shadow's neck.

"Who else can I trust if not you to look after the men until they are back on their feet? Their health could take months to recover, and I would not see them suffer any longer in the dungeon," Annora replied. She went to check the cinches but everything was in order.

"I am only one man, Annora. If Tashe orders our return to the depths of Meregate, we will easily be outnumbered. Some of us may even find our way into that damn pit. No one here will be able to come to our defense and you know it," Merek answered as he continued to frown.

As though Tashe knew he was the topic of their conversation, the man himself came from the keep and strode in her direction. Clearly, he had not taken her warning to heart and wished to further assert his claim to Meregate before she departed.

He took hold of her arm in a firm grip and pulled her close to him. "You presume much, woman. Do you think you can just return here and issue orders to me? Me! The man who was appointed steward?" Clifton hissed.

She reached behind her to pull out a dirk and pressed the blade against his fleshy belly. "Give me a reason not to plunge this into your side, you worthless cur," Annora warned pressing the tip so he could in no way doubt she would not hesitate. "Release my arm."

He pushed her away and rubbed at his side. "The King will hear of this offense to me. Mark my words."

Annora held the blade and pointed the weapon toward Tashe. "I am just as certain he will hear far more from me first." She put the blade away and then looked around the bailey. "This man is nothing but a steward here. I *will* return one day to reclaim my land. Until then, I have given orders to ensure my people remain safe and fed."

As cheer rose up whilst Tashe left angrily cursing her name until the keep door slammed shut behind him. Annora turned back to Merek.

"Keep them safe to the best of your ability, my friend, until I can return."

"I will do all in my power, Annora, but you know that such a request will most likely be easier said than it can be done," Merek replied with a fierce scowl set upon his brow.

"I know," she said with a heavy sigh. "I can only pray that some of my threats may give warning to Tashe to at the very least keep you and my knights out of the dungeon."

"I highly doubt such will be the case," he grumbled.

"Do your best and hopefully I will be back to set my home aright," Annora said whilst Merek helped her into the saddle.

"God speed, my lady," Merek said giving her a bow.

"May God watch over you," Annora said before she pulled on the reins and began to lead the men who came to escort her back into the service of Stephen.

It took everything in her power not to look back. Instead, she focused her eyes in a steady gaze upon the road ahead. The one person who had been with her for as long as she could remember no longer was at her side and the thought of not having her captain with her dampened her spirits. She tried to rally them with the reminder that he would look after Leif and Meregate in her absence. With that last thought, Annora knew that she had done all she could for those she had left behind, and so she looked ahead to what might await her in her future.

CHAPTER TWENTY-ONE

STEPPING OUT OF the keep, Richard saw that the inner bailey of Devizes Castle was filled with horses and knights. It appeared as though everyone was ready to travel. Many of those gathered would journey with Lord Robert and young Henry to Bristol, while others would accompany Oswin and Beatrix to Ashurst. The two groups would head in two totally different directions and Richard tried not to worry not only for Beatrix's safety but also for Henry who would one day be king.

Henry would continue his education alongside his cousin Roger who was one of Robert's younger sons. The Empress's son would remain at Bristol but would be able to still visit her on occasion at Devizes where she planned to remain instead of returning to Oxford.

Devizes was a strong stone fortress high on top of a motte and Empress Matilda would be well protected here. 'Twas not the palace from which she had intended to rule as queen of the land that had been her birthright from her father, but she seemed to have put that dream aside, accepting that the war to which she had devoted her years and her energies was not winnable. After all that had been won and struggled over and sacrificed, both sides were now more or less in the same position as when the battle for the crown began. It was as though Lincoln, Winchester, and Oxford had never happened.

But Devizes Castle was her own and the Empress could continue to make her plans in a place that would be her center of power, such as it was. All in all, Devizes was the perfect place for the Empress even though Richard still felt uncomfortable leaving others to watch over her. But she had made it clear where she wanted him to now go and he could not gainsay her edict.

Richard came out of his musings as he moved across the bailey. He came to his sister and the radiant smile she bestowed upon him told him much. She was indeed happy with her marriage to Oswin. Her home now was at Ashurst. One day, when Richard was finally allowed to return to his own home at Lyndhurst, he would be close enough to visit often. But would that day ever come? Any thoughts of settling down back at his parents' ancestral home—the one that would one day be his—seemed still to be far reaching.

Beatrix held out her hands to him and Richard pulled her into his embrace.

"Be well, little sister," Richard said, "and mind your husband."

She gave a light laugh at his words. "Oswin knows me well enough not to expect me to obey every command he thinks is in my best interest."

Oswin came and placed his arm around his wife's waist before placing a kiss upon her brow. "I will have my hands full with this lady," he teased her.

Richard chuckled. "I did try to warn you."

Oswin joined in with his own laughter. "Clearly since we are now wed, I did not heed your words."

Beatrix leaned her head on Oswin's shoulder. "'Tis too late now to recant your vows, my lord. You are mine and I will ensure you never forget it."

Oswin tipped her chin up to stare into Beatrix's eyes. "I look forward to the years together, my love."

Richard cleared his throat feeling as if he was intruding on what was turning into an intimate moment between the couple. "Safe travels to you both. I hope to see you soon, either at your home or Lyndhurst. Be sure to head there after you are settled to see mother and father. They will be disappointed they were not in attendance for your nuptials."

"We will," Beatrix replied, turning to look at Richard with a worried gaze in her brown eyes. She stepped forward to place a kiss upon his cheek. "I pray you will remain safe in your travels. Remember what I said about seeking out your own lady."

"I may not have such a luxury of requesting such an excursion but I will remember your words, sister," Richard replied and watched as Beatrix went to a wagon where the Empress's ladies in waiting awaited their own chance to give Beatrix their good wishes and farewells.

Oswin clasped his arm with Richard's. "Do not worry, brother. I will take good care of her."

Brother... aye. Oswin had already been a close friend but now Richard was truly related to one of his closest friends. It made him miss the Norwood brothers and the connection that they, too, had shared for most of their lives.

"God speed, Oswin, until our paths cross again."

"Watch your back, Richard," Oswin replied before he went to assist Beatrix into the wagon.

Richard went to his horse and saw that Lord Robert was ready to ride along with Henry who was already situated on his own horse.

"Lord Grancourt," Robert called. "Lead them out!"

"Aye, my lord," Richard declared as he motioned to the guards he would now command. "Let us away, men."

He rode his steed through the barbican gate of Devizes Castle knowing his time under the direct charge of the Empress was now over. 'Twould not take long to reach Bristol Castle and Richard was aware what awaited Henry once he reached his uncle's castle.

Richard would, of course, guard the young prince with his life if that was the duty demanded of him, but in truth, he had little idea of what awaited him at their destination. He had no notion if he would be left at Bristol to guard the young prince or if he would follow Lord Robert into his next battle. Since he had been appointed Captain of the Guard, Richard assumed he would follow Lord Robert. But the whims of men could be fanciful, and situations constantly changed when a war continued to rage. Only time would tell what would come next and Richard would have no choice but to allow others to decide his fate.

CHAPTER TWENTY-TWO

June 1143
The outskirts of Wareham

ANNORA RACED HER horse, following the knights in front of her as they made their escape from Wareham. Months of planning had given Stephen a new campaign, intended to strengthen his position in the west country. She had followed his army from one castle to the next. Stephen had set his sights on Wareham to lay siege to the castle and gain control of the city. Wareham was a main port controlled by Matilda to maintain communications to her husband in Normandy. But it turned out the city was well-guarded and its defense strong under the leadership of Robert of Gloucester. When Stephen's scouts returned with news that they were being pursued by Earl Robert's knights, Stephen and his army headed north to evade capture.

The horses in front of her began to slow and Annora gazed behind her to check for any enemy forces that still pursued them from behind. As far as she could see, the enemy knights had fallen off and were no longer giving chase. This gave their own horses time to rest as the company slowed their steeds into a walk. She turned to the man riding beside Shadow to share with him her concern.

"We could have easily been captured back there," she said with a frown. "I do not understand Stephen's need to invade this part of the land where Matilda's control is so strong."

Percival nodded leaning an arm on the saddle whilst they continued forward at a slower pace. "The King is a man on a mission as is

Matilda. These skirmishes are like a game between them as they hope to gain further land in their name. Both know that the war is reaching its conclusion and wish to have as strong a bargaining position as possible when it comes time to broker the terms of peace."

"I do not care that I am but a pawn controlled by others," Annora snapped looking ahead to where the King was commanding they halt. "What do you suppose is going on now?"

Percival gave a shrug and sat tall in his saddle again. "Who is to say? We are at the whim of a king."

"Ride ahead and see if you can find any news as to where we are headed next," Annora asked the knight who slapped the reins of his mount and went forward.

Manfred came to take his place next to her. "Do you suppose the King has changed his mind and determined that we might return to London?"

Annora sighed. "I highly doubt it. I have the feeling we will be using the strength of our sword arm before too long. He will have us fighting with our lives just to gain another small bit of land to control."

"Sometimes I fear we will never see home again," Manfred complained before he looked around him. "Not that I would leave the King's army. I am a loyal subject, after all."

A smirk lit Annora's face—the first in days. She knew Manfred and Percival's loyalty actually lay with the Empress much like her own. It seemed that they, too, were subject to the King's pleasure in order to ensure the protection of their families back home. Aye… the similarities between their situations were all too apparent. Just as they yearned to fly back to the arms of their families, she would also like to do nothing more than lay down her sword and return home to her son. But clearly, that was not to be as yet.

Percival came back. His face gave away his displeasure before he even opened his mouth.

Annora could only imagine the news he would bring her. "I suppose from your frown that your news will not bring us any comfort."

Percival shook his head whilst his frown remained fierce. "Nay. You will not be pleased."

"Out with it then. There is no point in putting off the inevitable," Annora ordered, waiting to learn of where they were headed next.

Percival sighed. "He is determined to sack Salisbury. We are to head to a small abbey in Wilton where we can take refuge. The King will plan his attack from there.

Annora and Manfred both swore, and a troubled glance passed between the three of them. The two men had become trustworthy friends. Stephen had chosen well when he appointed them to guard her... not that she could not look after herself. But in the heat of battle, 'twas always good to have someone watching your back and with Merek still at Meregate, these two men had more than proven their worth in the past several months in the role that had always been his.

"It should not take us long to reach Wilton, then, if that is where we are headed. Hopefully we can get our tents pitched before the night is upon us, otherwise we'll be spending the night on the ground."

Percival shrugged. "'Twould not be the first time..."

"...nor the last," Manfred finished.

"Let us away, men," Annora answered as the army began to move again.

Bringing up the rear of the company caused her to bring a cloth up to her nose to help her breathe through the dust. With an entire army riding in front of her, a dust cloud had formed that was at times unbearable. But she would continue to stand the torment of bringing up the rear. She actually preferred being out of direct eyesight of Stephen. Whenever she was requested to join him, he seemed to gain great pleasure in tormenting her with the threat of her return to Meregate taking years. Years! She could not bear being away from her son that long. But what could she do but maintain her position as a compliant warrior? But one day… one day she would find an opportunity to flee and return home to take control again.

Inwardly she sighed at the thought of what it would truly take for such a feat to be accomplished. She had no army of her own. No joining forces that would fight on her behalf. There was no one that would be running to her aid with the exception of the two knights who now rode with her. Merek she knew she could depend on but months had passed since they had parted ways, and only God above knew what his fate had been since then. She may have ordered Tashe to follow her commands, but she was not stupid. He probably had her men thrown right back in the dungeon the moment the gate closed behind her. Her situation was grim and there was not much light to brighten her hopes for her unknown future.

The memory of a man with the bluest eyes she had ever beheld flashed briefly in her mind. After all this time, even his parting vow that he would find her seemed like 'twas all only just a dream. And yet, as she laid to find her slumber each night, she offered up a prayer on his behalf. Not that he would come to her rescue but that he would find his own happiness. She could not give herself hope that such a fate would include her but she could not prevent her dreams each night from showing her the future as she wished it. And each morn when she awoke, a sadness filled her heart for what would never be…

CHAPTER TWENTY-THREE

RICHARD PULLED BACK on the reins of his horse whilst watching Stephen and Bishop Henry flee Wilton Abbey with a close guard surrounding them. *The cowards!* 'Twas clear that Stephen cared little for his lieutenants and their men whom he had left behind to be captured or killed, sacrificing them to ensure his own escape from Earl Robert's cavalry. Blake and Kingsley pulled their horses next to Richard's even as several knights drove their own horses forward in pursuit.

Richard gave his steed a pat on his neck to calm the horse down. His steed reared its front legs as if telling him to ride on. "Easy now, Noble," he whispered to settle him down. "There are more days ahead of us to chase after errant fools."

Blake pulled at the neck of his tabard whilst adjusting his position in his saddle. "You do not wish to pursue them?"

Richard shook his head. "Let the others give chase," he replied turning his horse back toward the camp where the battle continued to rage. "We shall return to the fighting and capture as many of Stephen's high-ranking officers as we can. If he is foolish enough to leave them behind, then he can pay the ransom to have them returned if they live after the battle."

Kingsley pulled his sword forward. "I am more than ready to fight these bastards."

Blake peered over to Richard. "Do you suppose *she* is among those fighting?"

Richard almost winced thinking of Annora taking her life in her hands. "'Twould make sense if she yet lives. Be on the lookout for her if you are able."

Kingsley lifted a brow even as a soft chuckle left his lips. "You are not planning on taking her hostage again, are you?"

That is *exactly* what Richard had in mind, but he did not voice his thoughts aloud. If he did espy Annora among those fighting, he would do all he could to ensure he kept her safe even if that meant he would fight by her side. He shook his head wondering how that would all work considering she would be fighting the earl's men. If he aided her, he would then be considered a traitor to the earl and Empress. He needed a clear head and thinking of the lady was not going to help him accomplish such an outcome.

"Just watch out for her," Richard snapped in frustration knowing he needed to keep himself alive so that he, too, would live another day.

The three friends returned to the battle scene. Richard rode Noble through the men on the ground using a mace to take down the enemy. He had the advantage of fighting from the height of his horse... that is until the enemy came at him from his own steed, causing Richard to fall to the ground. He would have returned to his faithful steed but the knight who unseated him swatted Noble on his rump, sending the steed off.

A sound behind him alerted Richard of an enemy, and he swiftly turned just in time to raise his shield to deflect a battle ax aimed at his body. The jarring force sent him momentarily to one knee, but he recovered quickly. He swung his weapon at the knight's legs and heard a howl of pain when it made contact. The knight fell and Richard moved on to the next man who came at him bent on taking his life.

There was always another enemy to take the place of one he had felled. Richard lost his mace and drew his sword, hacking his way through his enemies all in the name of Empress Matilda and Earl

Robert. Time ticked by until he briefly caught sight of a helmet flying from the head of a knight, revealing tawny hair in a long braid. He had found her.

Richard began fighting his way to Annora, stepping over bodies of the dead in his haste to reach her. "Annora!"

A grunt left him when someone elbowed him in his belly, and it took a minute for him to recapture his breath and search out the lady again. She gave him a wide-eyed expression of disbelief before plunging herself back into the battle. She was so driven with what was going on in front of her, that she did not realize there was a threat from behind.

"Annora! Behind you," Richard called, trying to run in her direction. But the ground was slick from the battle and between the mud and blood that soaked the ground, his footing was precarious.

Annora whirled around in time to deflect the blade that had been aimed at her back. With a few more swings of her weapon, she felled the knight trying to kill her whilst Richard at last reached her side.

"What the devil are you doing, Richard?" she bellowed with a scowl.

"I found you," Richard exclaimed but he was in a quandary because now he had no idea whom he should fight. If he were to protect Annora, he would be attacking the very men who served under his command. But joining those men in their attacks would mean turning his sword against Annora. Whilst that thought ran amuck in his head, he did the only thing possible. He took hold of her arm and began pulling her from the battlefield.

"Let go of me," she ordered, struggling to escape from his hold without any success.

"I need to get you out of here," Richard replied as he continued to pull her along.

"The hell you do," she snapped. "I have a duty to fulfill, or have you forgotten my purpose?"

Richard frowned as she continued to thrash against the grip of his fingers from her arm. "I have forgotten nothing. I, too, have a purpose that I cannot accomplish with you in my way. I need to save you."

"No one told you to do so and I can save myself," she hotly retorted. She kicked his shin that only stunned him briefly.

"If that is the best you can do to defend yourself, then 'tis good that I came when I did. Or did you forget that you would have had a sword buried into your back had I not called out a warning?" he retorted as he pulled her near a tree and let go of her arm. He looked around to ensure they were safe. For the moment, they were—but 'twas not a safety that would last for long.

"My thanks for that but I still do not need you to fight my battles," Annora declared sharply taking several steps backward away from him. "Now, if you will excuse me, I need to return to the fighting."

"Your fighting is over for the day. If you but cared to take a second to look about you, you would see that Stephen and the Bishop have fled, leaving you and their men to fight a losing battle. 'Tis only a matter of time before all is lost for Stephen's cause in this place."

She lifted her chin in defiance. "Then I will continue on and surrender when the rest of Stephen's army concedes."

"Foolish woman," he yelled before taking both of her arms and giving her a shake. "Do you want to die for a worthless cause?"

"You know I have my reasons for fighting for Stephen," she countered.

"And you know I cannot allow you to continue," Richard replied. The fighting was drawing closer, and he knew he would need to make a quick decision regarding Annora.

"You do not own me, nor do you have any say on what I do," she said, holding firm to her resolve.

"I do now," he said making his decision. He came to stand before her, yanking her sword from her hand after a brief tug-of-war between them. He quickly tucked her weapon in his belt. Bending down, he hoisted the protesting woman over his shoulder and began to carry her away from the battle.

"Put me down this instant, Grancourt, or I shall scream," she warned whilst pounding on his back with her fists.

"Go ahead. No one will hear you above the sounds of war," Richard answered as he continued to carry her away.

"I hate you!"

"Nay, you do not."

She began to curse him to hell whilst he completely ignored her outrage and the foul names she called him. As he continued carrying her away, Richard could only begin to wonder if the accord they had formed during their previous time together would ever be renewed. From the ire in her tone now, 'twas as if their kisses at Oxford never happened. Richard wished he could change their present situation. He was going to need to start all over again trying to tame this hellcat of a woman.

CHAPTER TWENTY-FOUR

THIS WAS *NOT* happening again! Pounding her fists on Richard back only earned her sore hands because of the chainmail he wore beneath his tabard. This foul beast presumed much as he continued carrying her farther and farther away from the battlefield. How dare he think he could just take over and control the outcome of her life? He had no right!

"Release me this instant, you bloody whoreson!" she yelled to no avail. Instead, he slapped her bottom as if she were a misbehaving child. "How *dare* you!"

He slapped her again but did so this time with a chuckle. "I will dare much where you are concerned, my lady," Richard answered as he adjusted her weight on his shoulder before he chuckled. "Have you gained weight since we last met?"

A roar of outrage rang from her lips. She pounded upon his back again. "You bloody bastard," she swore.

"I believe we already had the discussion, but in case you required a reminder—I am a titled lord so your name calling will get you nowhere. Now behave before you end up with a sore bottom."

She cursed again earning her another playful slap... not that his abuse hurt. Nay. 'Twas more like a tap to get his point across but still! "Put me down, Richard," she bellowed again until he finally listened to her demand and put her back on her feet. She swayed from the sudden movement, and he took hold of her arm to steady her. "You have no right!

"Aye, I do," Richard proclaimed folding his arms over his firmly muscled chest.

"You know why I must needs fight for Stephen," she argued but to no avail. The man before her was too stubborn for his own good.

"And you must know why I cannot in good faith allow you to continue to do so. It appears we are at a stalemate."

"Give me my sword so I might return to the fighting," she ordered holding out her hand.

"As I just said, your days of fighting for Stephen are at an end."

"You cannot make choices on my behalf when you know I fight for my son's life and the safety of those left at Meregate," Annora declared placing her hands upon her hips. How could he prevent her from fighting when the lives of her people and her son were at stake?

"I understand your plight, but you must also see my reasoning of why I cannot allow you to continue," Richard answered stepping closer causing her to inch backward. If he touched her now in any sort of intimate way, she knew her heart would crack.

"We are not wed, nor do you have any say on my life, Grancourt," she replied whilst attempting to hold onto her temper. Yelling seemed unlikely to gain her anything but another smack to her bottom. "You cannot just show up and assume control over me."

"We may not be betrothed as yet—"

"There is no *as yet*," she yelled at him. "Now give me my sword."

"—but 'tis my hope that we can perchance one day come to an agreement," he finished whilst standing there with a seductive smile plastered on his unfairly handsome face.

Did he honestly think one look at him would melt her resolve? From the slow smile that slid across his lips, that was exactly what he was thinking. Well, she would prove him wrong! She stepped closer hoping to pull her sword from his belt. He relaxed his stance and Annora assumed he thought she would give in to whatever plans he had for her. He began to lower his head and for the briefest instant she wanted to feel his lips upon hers—but that would only prove his point and not her own.

Her hands went to his chest to hold off any further advances from him. When she finally voiced her thoughts aloud, her tone was clear and strong. "I will *never* concede to whatever plans *you* think are in my best interest. I am perfectly capable of seeing to my own needs and the commitment I have made in order to return to my home and people."

Those hypnotic blue eyes widened at her words before his brows contracted. "I thought mayhap given our time at Oxford that you might favor a union between us."

"You mean the few *days* when you forced me to be in your company?" she retorted hotly.

He shrugged. "Days… weeks… what does it matter how much time has passed when there is some invisible connection between a man and a woman?"

"I hardly would say a few conversations were enough to conclude that we would suit one another for a lifetime together," she said knowing she was telling a falsehood. She would not think on their brief time together and how the memory of those days had held her heart and spirit together on the darkest of days since they were in each other's company.

Richard took hold of her arms and brought her closer. "Feel free to lie to yourself, Annora, but do not utter such falsehoods to me. I know what we shared even if you think you can easily dismiss the attraction."

"There was no attraction," she murmured, repeating the lie if only to try and convince herself.

A laugh left him. "Shall I prove it to you, my dear?"

"You would not dare!"

He took her chin and tilted her head up giving her no choice but to gaze upon him directly. "I believe, sweet Annora, that I have already proved I will dare much where you are concerned."

"I do not know why you are bothering at all with me. I am no one to you," she shouted in despair.

"You are *all* to me."

His words rocked her to her very core, and she could only stare at him with her mouth open. Hate him or love him, she still could not risk losing her home and son because of an infatuation with a handsome stranger. For that was what he was—a man who briefly came into her life and gave her hope for another path she could have taken before reason once again required her to take control of her present situation. He had been but a brief dream of a life that she knew would never become a reality.

"You barely know me," she said in a last effort to change whatever was about to happen.

"And we shall have plenty of time in the days ahead to get to know one another again," Richard declared with a smile. "I made a vow that I would find you one day and now I have. Do you honestly think I will easily let you go?"

"You must. People's lives are at stake, or have you forgotten about my son?"

"I have not forgotten anything you have told me about your son, Annora. And that, too, shall be resolved with time."

"You do not understand!" she bellowed. "I do not have time. If I do not report to Stephen's captain, I will forfeit all."

Richard stared at her with a worried frown. "You cannot report to someone if you have been captured."

"You are not seriously going to take me prisoner again, are you?" she snapped.

"How else will your absence be explained? Even now, Stephen has made his escape with Bishop Henry, leaving his men to be killed or captured. Now if you are done arguing with me, let us be on our way," Richard said waiting for her to concede.

"Nay."

One dark brow rose at her answer. "You will not go on your own accord?"

"Nay," she repeated crossing her arms over her chest.

"So be it." Richard came at her so quickly she barely had time to protest when he once again lifted her up and hoisted her over his shoulder. She placed her forearms on his back so her head would not thump against his back with each step he took.

"Richard!" Her attempt to protest her mishandling only afforded her another slap on her bottom.

"Hush! You had your chance to walk on your own. Now you must needs pay the price for your insolence in refusing to listen to me," Richard replied.

The sound of horses drawing closer only had Annora hiding her face in her hands knowing that others were nearby to witness her humiliation.

"Grancourt," a voice bellowed when the horses slowed to a walk next to Richard. "Why are you walking away from the battlefield when you are needed?"

"Just taking a prisoner, my lord," Richard replied as he continued walking.

"Then set the man down and allow him his dignity," the voice ordered, causing Richard to chuckle.

"This is no man, my lord, but a woman."

"Really?" the voice drawled in apparent fascination.

"Aye, my lord, and my prisoner," Richard exclaimed.

"And is she unable to walk on her own accord?"

"She is... *stubborn*, my lord."

"Ensure she is secured and will not escape before you return to the battle. The men need their captain," the man said before his horse went off in a gallop.

Annora continued to squirm trying to see where this insufferable man was taking her. From the tents they passed, she could make out that she was now deep within the enemy's camp. When he opened the flap to a tent, Annora assumed the structure belonged to Richard. He put her on her feet, and she quickly made a mad dash toward the entrance.

"Not so fast, Annora," Richard said with a sly grin. He grabbed her about the waist, and she twisted in his arms. That was probably a mistake on her part since she was now firmly held as his arms of steel brought them close. She firmly pressed her hands against the solid wall of male chest.

"Let me go," she insisted sharply.

"I thought we were past this part of the discussion and that you had realized your fate was sealed." He pushed her into the center of his tent and quickly went to grab a rope. Her eyes widened as she realized that he would actually tie her up to be held against her will.

"Nay!" she cried out.

"Aye," he retorted and pulled her to the center post before forcing her to sit upon the ground. He made quick work of tying her hands behind her back. She was at his mercy, and she did not care for the situation one bit!

"Oh, how I hate you for this," she muttered. If the glare she tossed him were daggers, he would be severely injured and bleeding from multiple wounds.

Richard knelt in front of her. "I think I mentioned before there is a fine line between love and hate. I look forward to proving that your hatred of me is far from the whole of your feelings for me."

He leaned forward and their breath mingled in the air between them before he gently placed his lips upon her own in a soft kiss. She turned her head to break the contact and heard him chuckle before he left her side and exited the tent.

Even without his presence, he left her with the lingering taste of his kiss upon her lips. Their brief contact had ignited a flame to all the feelings she had originally experienced with Richard whilst at Oxford.

Their connection, no matter how much she had tried to deny it, was still as real as the fact that he had taken her prisoner against her will... again.

Alone and angry, she could only ponder what she was to do now and more importantly, how she would escape.

CHAPTER TWENTY-FIVE

Richard, Blake and Kingsley stood at the back of Earl Robert's tent. The earl was contemplating the prisoners kneeling before him. Two were high ranking lieutenants in Stephen's army whilst the other ten were of lesser rank but still of high import to the usurper's cause.

"Take them away and ensure they cannot escape," Robert said with a wave of his hand. "We shall see what your supposed king is willing to sacrifice in order to gain your return to his ranks."

The earl's knights stepped forward and began dragging away the prisoners leaving only Richard and his two friends still in attendance. The earl waved him forward and Richard leaned over to whisper to Kingsley and Blake.

"Wait for me outside," he said. The two knights nodded and left. Richard stepped forward and bowed before Earl Robert.

"Tell me of the woman you captured. Who is she to you?" Robert asked holding out his hand whilst a servant placed a chalice in his palm.

"'Tis the Lady Annora de Maris, my lord," Richard answered before taking a seat in a vacant chair once the earl bid him to sit.

"And?" the earl drawled.

"She has been forced to serve King Stephen since his forces laid siege to her home of Meregate Castle. His men continue to hold her people and her son captive whilst she serves him," Richard answered evading the rest of the earl's question.

"Such is the fate of many castles and their people who have fallen under Stephen's control but that still does not tell me what the woman is to *you*, Grancourt," Robert said leaning forward in his chair. "Is she only your prisoner or is she more?"

"The Lady Annora is... more, my lord," Richard replied quietly. The earl waved again to a servant and a goblet of wine was offered to Richard that he gladly accepted. He had the notion he would need a drink to finish this conversation.

Robert sat back in his chair. "I assumed as much considering she wasn't brought before me with the rest of Stephen's men who he left behind to rot."

Richard nodded. "I am certain the king will pay a stiff penalty for the surrender of his men."

"A runner will be sent to find the coward so my terms can be presented," Robert agreed before continuing. "But tell me, Grancourt, what shall we do about Lady de Maris?"

Richard set down his cup on the small table next to his chair whilst he contemplated the earl's question. 'Twas a dilemma that had plagued him all day. He knew that, if given the chance, Annora would return to her service to Stephen if it meant her son would remain safe. But she could continue her service to the man for years before he might let her people and estate go free... that is, if she even lived long enough to achieve such an outcome. Her life could end just as abruptly as anyone's who fought in a pitched war.

"Richard..."

Richard looked up and realized he had been momentarily lost in thought whilst Earl Robert waited for Richard's reply. He had no notion what the earl had said. "My lord?"

"I just asked you what we can do to help your lady," the earl repeated with an amused grin.

Relief swept through Richard's mind knowing the earl would give aid where he could. "Meregate is a strong fortification on the coast and its people were loyal to the Empress before it fell into the hands of Stephen. Close to Dover, it would lend additional aid for any of the Empress's ships that need to dock on the coast. We could send men to lay siege to the place and take the castle back in the Empress's name."

"A siege is costly, Grancourt, as you are well aware. What makes you think we can take Meregate back?"

"Lady Annora can lend aid by giving insight into any weakness that the current steward may not know about. Although I have not had a chance to speak in depth with the lady on this topic, I believe she would agree to giving us aid since her son's life is at stake. Her husband was beheaded during the last siege. She would be a willing participant to seek revenge for his killing and to free her son and people from their captivity," Richard replied.

Earl Robert tapped his finger to his chin whilst contemplating Richard's words. "She will be considered a traitor to those who do not know her complete story. Giving her aid might also diminish your credibility as my Captain of the Guard."

"I am certain once the men learn of the injustice done to her and her family, they will unite to undo the wrong that has been committed," Richard answered honesty.

"If she is indeed willing to give us aid, her inside information could go a long way to shorten any siege we put into place," Robert proclaimed taking another sip of his wine.

"She will agree," Richard clearly stated.

"You seem certain of the lady's answer. If this is the case, then I will lend my support and provide you with the men needed to return Meregate to its rightful owner. Go and have a talk with your lady and then report back to me as to her answer. We shall make further plans if she agrees to lend aid where needed."

"My thanks, my lord," Richard said coming to a stand. He gave the earl a bow and left the tent with Blake and Kingsley falling into step with him.

"Are we giving chase with the runner?" Kingsley asked.

"Nay. Others will handle the ransom of the king's men," Richard replied as he picked up his pace.

"Where do we head next?" Blake inquired with a frown. "If we are not racing after that cowardly king, then what does the earl expect of us?"

"Aye! Being idle and doing nothing wears on my pride when I feel like we should be fighting for our Empress," Kingsley added.

Richard halted and turned to his friends. "I must needs speak with Lady Annora. If she agrees, you may have the next battle in your hands sooner than expected."

He left Blake and Kingsley who were only too happy with the knowledge that another battle would be within their grasp. Richard was glad to see the knight he'd assigned to watch his tent was still standing guard at the entrance. He dismissed the man and entered.

Richard's gaze swept the dimly lit interior and came to rest on the lady whose green eyes flashed her resentment. Even from this short distance, Richard could see for himself that the woman's anger had not cooled in the brief time since they parted. He supposed leaving her tied up like he had did not endear him to her.

Scanning the rest of the small tent, he made his way over to a corner where a chamber pot sat. He made quick work of assembling a makeshift curtain for her privacy so she could take care of her business. When he stood over Annora, she tipped her head back so she could stare directly into his face. Her glare was mutinous.

"If you give me your word you will not try to escape me, I will release you from your bonds," Richard said wondering if he could trust her long enough to have a civil conversation with her about his plans. She said nothing, which only continued to prove how angry she was. "Your word, Annora."

"Aye. I give it," she finally replied and he went to untie her hands. He offered his hand to help her rise. He should not have been surprised when she slapped it away. He motioned to the closed off area and Annora made her way there, remaining behind the curtain until she was finished and stepped back out to face him.

"I have news," Richard began motioning to a stool at the table.

"I am certain you do. Does your bloody earl mean to make an example of me and the other officers who are loyal to King Stephen?" she inquired as she remained standing with her hands behind her back.

"Sit down, Annora," Richard said firmly.

"Nay."

"Do you plan to fight me on everything?" he asked wearily.

She cocked her head to one side as if in disbelief. "Are you surprised when you hold me hostage yet again?"

He gave a heavy sigh. "Nay. I suppose not," he replied before making another attempt. "Please take a seat, Lady Annora."

Her resolve seemed to lessen at that courtesy as though some of the fight had gone out of her. He hated to see her dispirited but their next conversation was of major import and would decide the fate of her people. She finally sat on the stool and Richard pulled another next to her.

"I have spoken to Earl Robert," he began before she cut off his words.

"I am surprised that I am not dead at the end of his sword," she said through clenched teeth.

"The earl is not someone who unjustly goes about killing innocent people no matter what you might have heard of his reputation," Richard said defending the man.

"Then what part am I to play in returning to my place in Stephen's army?"

He gave another sigh. "As I told you earlier, you are no longer to serve as a part of his armed forces. I cannot have you killing the earl and Empress's men in your fight against your perceived enemies."

"Perceived? They *are* my enemies as long as Stephen holds Meregate and my son captive," she bellowed slamming her fist on the table. "Why cannot you understand the role I must play in order to see to my son's release?"

Richard reached over to take her hand but she pulled back refusing to accept any comfort he might offer her. So be it. "Let us speak honestly between ourselves, you and I." He waited a moment and saw that her anger appeared to have cooled before he continued with his harsh words of wisdom. "You could spend the rest of your life fighting for Stephen and living by the strength of your sword until your effort to remain loyal to him kills you. Even in death, Stephen would never release your son."

Hurt flashed across her features along with bitter resignation, as if she had already considered such a possibility. "You do not know that," she finally answered but she could not hide from him the quiver of her chin that proved she knew he was right.

"I do. Any man who would flee a battle with only his most trusted knights to ensure his escape has no loyalty to those he leaves behind. That you were not among those knights should tell you of your worth in his eyes."

"But he told me—"

"He told you what you needed to hear in order to ensure you adhered to his demands," he said quietly. This time when he reached for her, she allowed him to take her trembling fingers. He cupped his hands over hers.

Her head fell forward in defeat. Some of her tawny tresses had come lose from her braid and shielded her face. Richard heard her heavy sigh as though she had at last accepted the reality of her situation. When she lifted her head, tears slid down her cheeks. He lifted a hand and ran his thumb over the wetness hoping this small gesture might give her some comfort.

"The King still has my son and people. What am I to do?" she asked him whilst her tone spoke of the concern she had for those she had left at Meregate.

"Do you trust me?" he inquired, waiting anxiously for her answer.

She let out a weary sigh. "Why should I trust you or any other man after what you just told me?"

"You should trust *me* because of this..."

Richard leaned forward slowly, giving her the opportunity to prevent him from getting any closer to her. Brilliant green eyes searched his blue ones for the truth of his words. Since she didn't halt his forward motion, he continued bending forward until his lips touched her own in a gentle kiss. Her hands reached out to clasp his forearms as if his support was the only thing keeping her upright. Richard's desire for her was as strong as ever, but he would not push her further. He broke off their brief contact much to his regret. Richard continued to stare upon her face that showed her emotions still warred within her.

"What do you propose?" she reluctantly asked him. She did not profess she trusted him but Richard took this as a sign that they just might agree to a common accord—at least for now.

"We have a plan..."

CHAPTER TWENTY-SIX

THE BRIEF BATTLE between Stephen and Earl Robert's men at Wilton did not last long. Although Richard had informed Annora that she was no longer his prisoner, a guard had still been placed at the entrance to his tent. *So much for trust* had been her first thought, but when she fully considered her situation, she had to admit that she did not blame Richard for being wary of her. His plan to lay siege to her home in order to return the estate into the control of the Empress had many points at which it could fail. Whilst she had left Merek to ensure her son's safety, she could not say that even now her captain was not residing in the castle's pit—or in a grave.

For nigh unto a week, she had remained inside Richard's tent. Since they last met, he had been appointed Captain of the Guard for Earl Robert. A prominent position and one he took with great seriousness. Men came to him throughout the day and he listened intently to their words before forming his opinion on the matters that needed his attention. He was fair with those who came to him, Annora had to admit as she listened to all he dealt with.

But this did not mean she would allow herself to be swayed so easily by Richard's kind and flowery words. Or so she kept telling herself as she continued to remain in the confinement of a tent that seemed to get smaller and smaller as each day folded into the next. At night whilst they supped, Richard would tell her of his life at his home at Lyndhurst or his exploits with the Norwood brothers once they joined the Empress's cause. The deep, rich baritone of his voice lulled her into a sense of security that she had not felt in many a year and the ice surrounding her heart cracked open a little more somehow letting the man in.

The nights had been the worst as she laid for hours tossing and turning unable to sleep knowing Richard was close. His soft breathing haunted her every waking hour and when she did finally manage to drift off, images of a handsome knight with the bluest eyes she had ever beheld made her yearn in desire until she awoke more frustrated than ever before.

When Richard came to inform Annora they would begin packing up their camp and make their way toward Meregate, Annora was relieved but also worried for her people. A siege could last for months. What would happen inside the castle to her people and son before Clifton Tashe might be forced to surrender? Annora was certain he would not give up easily, or quietly, and she did not relish the fact that starving out Tashe might easily harm her own son and remaining people loyal to her household as well.

The sound of the tent collapsing as the men continued their work brought Annora out of her musings. She did not know what her future held except for the hope that her home would again be returned to her. But even that thought held a bit of uncertainty. When she was once again lady of her castle, she would need to take a husband, that much was clear. With the exception of Richard, there was no other who she might petition to marry her.

"Lady Annora, we are here to take you to Richard," a voice said pulling her again out of her thoughts.

She raised her head to stare at two knights. One with black hair and the other blond. She stood and tilted her head to one side. These two had been at Oxford. She was certain she had seen them training that day when she had confronted Richard.

"Since we shall be riding and fighting together, might I know your names?" she asked while she rocked on her heels waiting for them to reveal their identities.

The one bearing black hair and green eyes spoke first. "Blake Kennarde, at your service, my lady," he said with a short bow of his head.

"Kingsley Goodee," the other replied also giving her a bow.

Annora gave them a small smile. "Since I am to be escorted to Grancourt, we best not keep the man waiting."

As she walked between the two towering men, she could not help but realize how small in stature she truly was compared to these warriors. That they would join her cause gave her further consideration of what everyone involved might hope to gain or might lose. She kept her silence as they continued to press forward until she saw Richard standing by the side of a man who she assumed was the Earl of Gloucester. Since she had not been formally introduced to the earl, she had no way of knowing his identity.

When she began to draw closer, she came to the sudden realization that there were at more than a dozen men she recognized as being loyal to King Stephen. She had fought beside them, shared meals with them, heard the tales of their lives. Though she had no love for their leader, sadness momentarily filled her knowing these knights were being held for ransom. Two in particular caught her attention and she knew she needed to have a private word with Richard in order to gain the men's freedom. Since she had barely spoken to Richard in the past se'nnight, even though he had prattled on each night, she would likely need to put forth an extra amount of effort to be cordial if she wanted to convince him to have the men released. They had been loyal to her over the past several months and had watched her back. That in itself was enough for Annora to plead their cause.

She bobbed a curtsy before the two men. "My Lord Grancourt..." she began, whilst plastering a smile on her lips. "If I might have a brief moment of your time?"

Richard looked away from the man he had been talking to and one dark brow rose as though in amusement at the overly sweet tone of her voice. Inwardly she cursed knowing she had perchance put a little too much emphasis on the pitch. Richard returned his attention back to the lord whose attempt to hide his own sense of amusement failed.

"My lord, may I present to you Lady Annora de Maris of Meregate," Richard said introducing her. She dropped down into a ladylike curtsy despite the fact that she was dressed in hose, tunic, and boots. "Lady de Maris, this is Robert, Earl of Gloucester."

"My lord. I cannot thank you enough for coming to the aid of my people," she said. 'Twas no small undertaking to lay siege to a castle and would cost this man greatly both in men and resources, representing a major loss to his coffers.

"Finally, I meet the legendary Lady de Maris," the earl crooned softly. "I have heard much from Grancourt of your exploits both at Winchester and Oxford, my lady."

Annora glanced between the two men, wondering just how much Richard had confided in the earl. "I only did what I must, my lord, in order to protect my son and home."

"And now you return your fealty back to Empress Matilda?" Earl Robert inquired whilst his face went from amusement to stern seriousness.

"Aye, my lord." Annora bobbed another curtsy for truly what other choice did she have but to agree to their terms? This may be her one and only chance to free Meregate and Leif. With the hopes of that freedom ahead of her, 'twas not hard to return her loyalty back to the Empress where it originally belonged.

Silence stretched between the threesome until the earl seemed satisfied with her answer. "Get the men moving toward Meregate, Richard," the earl ordered before his eyes swept the mayhem of the camp as the knights continued their work. "With the number of knights and all this gear, the journey make take well over a se'nnight before we reach the shore."

"Aye, my lord." Richard bowed whilst Annora gave another short curtsy. Once the earl left them, Richard finally turned to gaze upon her. "You wished to have speech with me, Annora?"

"Aye." She fumbled with the words to ask for a favor when she was well aware that Richard owed her nothing. She finally decided that speaking honestly would be her best approach. "There are two of Stephen's men who are being held that I would like to be released into my keeping."

A chuckle left him. "Did you not consider that perchance 'tis a little soon to be making demands of me?"

"'Tis more like a favor. Besides… this could be the start of coming to a common accord of a… personal nature between us. A token of good faith, so to speak," she murmured softly whilst pondering the fact that she was not sure her heart could stand being broken again.

"That remains to be seen," he replied gruffly sounding annoyed with her. But mayhap 'twas not necessarily her request that irked him so much as the prospect of all he must do to get the earl's men moving. "What makes you think I would allow two of Stephen's men to go free to return to killing my men?"

"They would not be going free if they remained by my side to watch over me. They are loyal to the Empress and have been fighting beside me since I left Oxford. They have watched my back in my Captain's stead since I left Merek Baringar at Meregate to look over my home in my absence."

His dark brow rose again at her words. "You do realize you most likely left Baringar to be taken and thrown into your dungeon."

"Merek knew the risks, but I needed someone I could trust to ensure my son was kept safe," she answered.

"And just how was Baringar to do this if he was held below? Or worse, if he was thrown into the castle's pit?" he asked folding his arms over his chest.

Annora gave a heavy sigh. "'Tis something that I have considered many times over the past several months, but what better options were available to me? I worry over the fate of my people and son with every breath I take."

"We shall be there soon enough and will do our utmost to return Meregate to its rightful owner," Richard proclaimed until he turned to look at the group of men. "Which ones will you vouch for?"

She had not realized she was holding her breath until the air rushed from her lungs in relief that Richard would fulfill her request. She described the two men and Richard called to one of the guards watching over the group of prisoners. He issued his orders and just as quickly, the two men were brought before Richard.

"This is Percival Ford and Manfred Crump, Lord Grancourt," Annora said grateful that the men would be released. "They have watched over me during many battles."

Richard remained silent for several minutes whilst inspecting the two men. He then nodded to the guard who quickly took a knife and cut the ropes binding the men's hands. "Lady de Maris has spoken highly of you and assures me that you are loyal to Empress Matilda and her cause. Is this so?"

Percival nodded. "Sometimes a person is forced into service against their will, my lord, as the lady herself is very much aware of."

"I trust them, Richard," she said, her use of his given name causing him to turn his full attention once again toward her. Those blue eyes delved deeply into her own green ones, and she swore they bore directly into her very soul.

"Let us hope I do not regret my decision to set them free." Richard looked behind them and waved his hand. "Blake and Kingsley... oversee them and ensure they do not get into any trouble. Lady Annora says they can be trusted to watch over her back but I would see such loyalty for myself before I, too, believe their worth."

"What shall happen to the rest of the men?" she asked wondering at their fate.

Richard quirked his brow. "They will be held in ransom and perchance they will be set free in exchange of Meregate's surrender."

Annora nodded knowing she could not do more for the other knights she had fought beside. She watched her two men as they began to follow Blake and Kingsley but not before Manfred's lips silently mouthed the words *thank you*. Turning back to Richard, she gave him a bright smile. "I appreciate the kindness you offered them."

"And what reward will you give me, Annora, for such a kindness?" he asked stepping close to her.

She stepped back knowing that if he touched her, 'twould be her downfall, especially given the dreams she had of him of late. "I did not realize I would have to forfeit something in return, Grancourt. A kindness given freely holds more worth than one that is expected to be repaid," she said not hiding her sarcastic tone.

A corner of his lip turned upward. "I think I liked it more when you called me by my given name."

"A mistake that I assure you will not happen again."

"I would have hoped that such a favor would be freely given as you just mentioned."

She tilted her chin up in order to fully stare upon this handsome man who was still such an enigma to her. "For something to be freely given requires the two of us to trust one another. We are barely on speaking terms. I do not think our relationship, such as it is, has yet to come to such a point that I even consider us friends."

"And yet I see the conflict in you each time we are together. Say you are indifferent to me all you like, Annora, but I know you care for me on some level." He stepped closer and leaned down to whisper in her ear. "Or else you would not whisper my name in the middle of the night whilst you sleep." He stepped back to watch her reaction to his words.

Her eyes went wide in alarm causing his smile to broaden. Before she knew what he was about, he again bent forward and placed a quick kiss on her temple. She swore her skin burned from where his lips had momentarily touched her skin.

She could find no sharp retort to lash back at him, nor could she deny the obvious with the now-arrogant knight. Instead, she remained silent, and Richard, likewise, said nothing more. Taking her numb arm, he began leading her toward her horse. Once she was settled in the saddle, Richard went to his own steed and swiftly mounted the animal as he began moving out the troops.

It wasn't until several miles had been put behind them that two things registered in her poor feeble mind. First, Richard had somehow found her horse Shadow, another item to add to the growing list of things she owed him for. The second was far more disturbing... Richard was very much aware that Annora's dreams had been filled with him. God help her!

CHAPTER TWENTY-SEVEN

ANOTHER LOG WAS thrown onto the campfire and sparks of red embers floated upwards, disappearing into the dark night sky. There was a low hum of male voices and laughter in the distant encampment as the men began settling down for the eve. Richard crossed his outstretched legs at his ankles in an attempt to get more comfortable. 'Twould not be the first time he'd slept without the comforts of his tent, and this night would certainly not be his last before they reached Meregate and whatever fate awaited them at Annora's home.

The lilt of soft laughter that was clearly feminine sounded out of place amidst all his knights, but it still caused a shiver of desire to rush through his entire body knowing Annora was so close. Richard could not deny himself the pleasure of staring across the fire to the lady who had all but consumed his thoughts since they first encountered one another. Months of yearning for a woman he barely knew had caused him much anguish. To now have her this near without having leave to touch her was almost unbearable. His deepest desire was to take her into his embrace and kiss her senseless, but he would never do such a thing without her consent, and she had been anything but welcoming since her capture. He would have thought he had imagined their brief connection whilst at Oxford had it not been for her whispered words whilst she lay slumbering in his tent.

Aye... when he had first heard his name called out to him in the dead of night from across his tent, he had jerked up from his own slumber to see what had been amiss. But there had been nothing to be alarmed about other than the restless tossing and turning of the woman who had woken him from his own troubled dreams and nightmares. How many nights had he stood over her wishing she would admit they had some sort of connection? He supposed he could not blame her for being wary of his motives given he had been forced to abduct her against her will *again*. Once had been bad enough. To have to have done so a second time caused everything within Richard to revolt. He had lived his entire life by a code of chivalry that he continued to break where Annora de Maris was concerned.

And yet what choice had he had when she had refused to see reason? He supposed he could have handled the situation differently, but once he had witnessed her almost getting herself killed at Wilton, his only thought had been to get the lady as far away from the battlefield as he could by any means necessary. He had thought by spending some time together, Annora might finally let her guard down where their relationship was concerned. He might as well have wished to be given wings so he could fly up to the heavens. Thus far, every attempt he had made had failed. She was just as stubborn as she had always been and nothing had changed for the better. In fact, now that she had her two knights with her again, she appeared to distance herself even further from him.

He threw another log on the fire before his gaze traveled to her once more as she again laughed with her men. Even Blake and Kingsley joined in with her merriment and Richard could only ponder what part of their conversation he had missed while he had been deep in thought and not attending to their words. He had never been one to be jealous of another man and yet that green-eyed monster had recently begun to rear its ugly head the more Annora ignored him and gave her attention and her smiles to others.

He decided that mayhap trying to find his slumber might be preferable to being miserable watching her amusement with others that he was no part of. He reached behind the log he was leaning against for his bed roll. The hour was growing late and the morn would be upon them sooner than he would have liked. Whilst he was busy unrolling his bedding for the night, the other knights took this as a sign that their relaxing conversations should come to an end. Blake and Kingsley disappeared beyond the light of the fire. Manfred and Percival did the same although Percival told Annora that they would be close in case she had need of them.

She bid the men a good night and she stated she would see them on the morrow before she, too, began preparing herself for her slumber. Once she and Richard had both settled themselves down, the silence stretched uncomfortably between them. Although they were not that far away from one another, Richard felt the distance might as well have been like the whole length of England. He rolled over on his side and took note that Annora had also placed her bedding so she could see Richard beyond the ring of the campfire. Perchance this was a good sign that she wished to know he was near.

He took notice that her green eyes were wide open whilst she intently watched him. Her face took on a rosy hue from the reflection of the flames of the fire as the logs were consumed down to a reddish glow of dying embers.

"You are in a most foul mood, Richard," she said softly placing one hand under her cheek. "What is troubling you?"

"'Tis nothing," he managed to mutter knowing this was far from the truth.

A light laugh escaped her and the sound caused his heart to beat a rapid staccato. "If 'tis nothing, I would hate to think how you will appear when something of great import is at hand."

He leaned up on one elbow before he finally voiced his thoughts aloud, all the while knowing that he should remain silent on the matter. "What are those two men to you?"

"Percival and Manfred?" she asked whilst she also raised up on one arm. A frown marred her otherwise lovely brow.

"Of course, I meant Ford and Crump," he mocked in frustration. "I do not think you had time to form any sort of a relationship with my men Kennarde or Goodee."

Her lips silently moved as though trying to form a response before she sat up fully, crossing her legs beneath her. Her frown deepened before her mouth opened in an O of surprise as though a revelation of great import had been revealed to her. "I cannot believe it," she declared with a slight grin. "You are jealous of them!"

"I said no such thing." He rolled over onto his back, crossing his arms over his chest to stare up at the midnight sky.

"You are!" She clapped her hands and Richard heard her muffled laugh.

By Saint Michael's wings! How would he ever live down this embarrassment was beyond him. "I am not jealous," he stated again hoping she would let the matter rest. Given his past conversations with this lady, he should have known she would never let it go that easily. He was so lost in his own self-made agony that he had not realized she had come over to him until she sat next to him.

She placed her hand on his arm and those same tingling currents raced up his body at her touch. "You have nothing to be jealous of, Richard. They mean no more to me than any other knight." Her voice had an underlying tone that pulled at his heartstrings. Could he dare to hope that mayhap she would at last admit there was something between them?

He was tired of feeling as though he was nothing but a barbarian whenever she was around. And yet she had a hold on him as no other woman in his past could ever claim. Mayhap that was why he was still drawn to her. She was different than the grasping women of court who were only interested in his wealth and title he would one day inherit once his father passed on from this world. He was beginning to feel that all of his defenses had tumbled down where this lady was concerned. She made him vulnerable in many ways, and perchance this was why she stood out.

He came to a sitting position next to her and hesitantly reached out to tuck a stray lock of her tawny hair behind her ear. "If you say this is the case, then I will assume you speak no falsehood," he declared. He would not let the emotion of jealousy get the better of him, not when Annora had taken this first important step.

"I may say many things that are unpleasant during the heat of the moment when we argue but I would never lie to you," she said whilst a small smile of encouragement lit across her visage.

A short chuckle left him. "Perchance you have spoken a falsehood or two when we spar," he replied whilst watching her carefully as he tried to find a way to pull down the rest of her defenses.

"Perchance. A woman does need to keep a few secrets to herself, my lord," she purred sweetly and his heart lurched inside his chest at how she teased him.

"There may be many things you use in your attempts to remain indifferent to me, Annora, but I can see past them. Your emotions play across your face as if they are clearly inscribed upon parchment," he declared quietly. He took hold of her hand and since she did not pull, he held tight.

She lowered her green eyes and he could see for himself she was embarrassed. "I suppose since you already mentioned you heard me whispering your name in the night that there is not much I can keep to myself any longer."

He ran his thumb across the top of her hand. "Surely you must know I care for you, my lady. I made a vow to you back at Oxford and I held true to my declaration to do everything within my power to see you safe when we met again. Surely you cannot fault me for that."

She at last raised her head to look upon him and he swore there was a hint of love shining in those depths. "You did hold true to your word, Richard. Aye, I cannot fault you for your chivalrous vow but yanking me from the battlefield might have cost me all I hold dear. Certainly, you cannot find fault in *me* for fighting to stay true to the vow *I* made to my son and Meregate's people."

"Nay. I can only admire you more which is why I pleaded your cause to the earl. Taking back Meregate fits in with the Empress's plans to retake as many castles as possible. It did not take much to convince him to move in that direction."

"I am thankful for your support," she whispered whilst a tear ran down her cheek, "and the earl's."

He raised his hand to brush the tear aside. "I promise I will do all in my power to free your son, Annora."

"Because taking back Meregate fits in with the Empress's plans?" she asked quietly. He heard the catch in her voice, betraying her fear that this was the only reason why he had pleaded her cause.

"Because I care for you," he repeated. "I would have thought you would know this by now but I suppose 'twill take time to prove myself to you," he replied. He could not hide the brief bit of disappointment he felt at her ongoing doubts.

He was surprised when she reached out her hand to cup his cheek. She searched his face as though she sought the truthfulness of his words. She rose up on her knees and Richard understood that the time had come for her to return to her pallet. But before she did so, she leaned forward and ever so gently placed her lips on his own. It took everything in his power not to take hold of her and take more.

"I care for you, too, Richard."

She quickly rose to her feet and went back to her own space by the fire. This time she turned away from him. Mayhap this was for the best. If he had to stare at her again for any longer, he just might forget the vow he had made to himself to give her time so they might come to a common accord.

But Richard now had hope. This eve had been a good beginning to their journey together.

CHAPTER TWENTY-EIGHT

ANNORA WOKE WITH a start and jerked herself upright before scanning her surroundings for any signs of danger. 'Twas an automatic response from living on the edge for so many years. But the camp was still quiet. From the looks of the sky, dawn was possibly fast approaching. She pulled the blanket closer to her chin even though she was warm from the fire at her backside. She wanted to stay oblivious to where her dreams had taken her but she could hardly deny what her heart was already telling her. She was madly in love with Richard Grancourt.

Such a realization, if only to herself, gave her cause to smile and as she did so the memories of her dreams caused her to shiver in delight. She could only imagine how the sensation of being held in strong arms would fill her with desire when it happened whilst she was awake rather than in her dreams. And the pleasure to be found when their bodies were skin to skin? A shiver of delight filled her at the mere thought of it. Annora squirmed on her pallet trying her best to get comfortable but who was she kidding? She had been fighting the memory of Richard since they left each other at Oxford and even though he had taken her captive again, her heart, in truth, rejoiced that he had found her.

Aye, after last night she would finally admit what her heart had known all along. She and Richard were destined for one another. Only a fool would deny oneself the knowledge that they had found the other half of themselves that had been missing. With a new resolve in her mind, she turned around to tell him what she had been feeling but disappointment filled her. Richard was gone from his pallet. She could only assume he was scouting the perimeters of the camp. It would explain why the fire was once more ablaze. He had ensured she would be warm once she awoke from her slumber. Richard had assumed this responsibility since the start of their journey, after informing the knight guard he would tend their fire. She smiled thinking of this small kindness he performed for her each eve and morn.

Since the majority of the knights were still asleep as far as she could tell, Annora decided now was the best time to take care of her personal business. She had learned long ago that privacy was a luxury that continually was a challenge traveling with a large group of men. She had seen glimpses of a river prior to making camp and after days in the saddle, she would not mind the chance to scour the dirt from her flesh. She would take advantage of this opportunity to bathe in private. She reached for her satchel, finding a drying cloth, along with the last bit of soap she still owned. Rummaging in the bottom of the bag unearthed relatively clean clothes. She did not have many left.

With her few belongings secured in her arms, she rose from the hard ground and began making her way through the trees. Stumbling on an unforeseen tree root, she began to pitch forward but caught herself before she fell to the forest floor. Cursing at her stupidity for not bringing a torch to light her way, she continued onward on her quest for a bath no matter how frigid the water might be.

She had expected to be alone as she broke through the tree line toward the river's edge. But the sight that met her eyes was one she would not soon forget. As though she still slept, the clouds above parted and the remaining moonlight shone down on the naked man rising from the water like a Greek God come to tempt her to sin. Aye... 'twas as if Poseidon had taken human form. All Richard needed was a trident to rule over the waters he stood in.

He pushed back the wet black tresses of his hair but 'twas his smoldering blue eyes when he espied her that caused her mouth to go dry. Annora could in no way mistake the look of desire that rushed across his face. She knew that she could quickly turn about and leave the man to finish his morning rituals in peace. 'Twas what she should have done… but instead, she found herself continuing to gawk at the fine body of Richard in all his naked glory.

She licked her lips, and a hint of a smile lit the corner of her mouth. Annora had been certain that Richard would be just as magnificent without his garments as he was within them, and he did not disappoint. Her eyes all but devoured his broad shoulders and arms of steel. His well-developed chest and a stomach rippling with muscles made her fingertips itch to touch his fevered skin. Lean hips and… well… 'twas a shame the rest of him was hidden from her view beneath the water. She could only imagine his manhood rising to the occasion of taking her.

Richard stretched forth his hand in an unspoken suggestion for her to join him. 'Twould be poor judgement on her part to accept such an offering. But to deny him would also be to deny herself and the feelings she had just reconciled within herself but moments before. There was no point in putting off the inevitable.

She dropped the bundle she had been carrying to her feet. Her boots came next and still Richard did not move but only waited for her in the waist deep water. Her hose, tunic and undergarments came next before she at last came to the water's edge. Her whole body ached in longing and for what awaited her but a short distance away. And still Richard waited for her to decide her own fate even though she had already done so by not leaving in the first place.

She shivered at the coldness of the water as she began to make her way toward him. And when he again stretched forth his arm, her hand easily was placed within his cool palm. Richard pulled her quivering body into his own and she inhaled sharply when her soft body was molded into the ruggedness of the man before her. How many nights had she envisioned his skin intimately touching her own? He pressed her closer, and her dreams became a reality.

"Annora…" Her name, whispered from those lips she wished to kiss, came out in a hoarse croak. 'Twas as though he could barely restrain himself and she was inwardly happy that she had such an effect on this handsome warrior. "Am I dreaming of you?"

She placed her fingertips on his lips. "Nay. You are certainly as awake as I am, Richard," she began before winding her arms around his neck. "But no words, for now. Love me as I have dreamed about since I met you."

"Are you certain? I do not wish you to regret our coupling come the morn," he said as if grappling with her decision to stay.

"The morn is almost upon us, and I will regret nothing, Richard. Love me," she crooned softly in his ear.

"I do, Annora," he replied, and he placed a crushing kiss upon her lips.

In that moment, they connected in an age-old ritual of lovers found. He carried them into deeper water and Annora could do nothing but hold onto the lifeline that was all Richard. Wrapping her legs around his waist, she tilted her head to one side so she might take advantage of the intoxicating kiss that seemed to breathe life into her. Their tongues intertwined in a dance she had craved in the very deepest recesses of her body. A low moan of pleasure escaped her, and she shivered in anticipation of what would soon occur between them.

"You are cold," he said after tearing his lips from her mouth.

"I am far from cold, my lord," she replied with an encouraging smile as she traced his lips with one fingertip.

"I see I may have awakened the temptress in you, my dearest Annora. What am I to do with you now?" His own cocky grin spread across his face, proving that he was well aware of the answer to his query.

"I am certain you will think of something, Richard."

"This is not exactly the way I would have initially made love to you. You deserve better."

"Desperate times means we must needs take advantage of our situation when 'tis presented to us." She pressed her body into his own and she heard his own low moan resonate from deep inside his chest. "I do not mind the unusual place for our coupling. In fact, I believe this adds to the excitement."

"You little minx," he teased her as he lifted her about her waist. "I believe the years ahead of us will be most pleasant, my love."

She only barely heard his endearment before he slowly lowered her down onto his manhood. A gasp escaped her as he filled her core and then stilled, giving her the time to adjust to the sheer size of him. Once again, Annora realized Richard did not disappoint. Once she had acclimated herself, he began to help her move in a rhythm known to lovers throughout all eternity. As the pleasure blossomed through her, she swore she would never be parted from this man again.

One hand cupped the back of his head and intertwined with his wet hair. Lost to anything else that was going on between them, she poured every ounce of feeling into ensuring this man might know how much he meant to her. Richard seemed to be in no hurry and yet Annora only wished for the release she knew would soon overtake her.

"You are mine," he growled out in a strained tone. "Say it…"

"Aye… I am yours as you are mine," she pledged. "Make me burn for you, Richard."

He gave no response other than to give in to her command by quickening their pace until Annora felt that she was on the edge of something incredible. And still Richard held back until her resolve at last broke. She shattered calling out his name as a force like white hot lightning wracked her body. Only then did he, too, reach his peak, spilling his seed within her.

When their breathing at last returned to normal, Richard kissed her forehead and then commanded her to stay where she was. He went to the bank of the river and returned with soap in hand, then he began to clean her body in a loving caress as the bar slid across her fevered skin. She wanted him again, but one look upwards told her much. Daylight was fast approaching. Their stolen moment to be alone together was coming to an end.

Once she was cleaned to his satisfaction, he took her hand, and they made their way to the edge of the river. They began to dress in silence, not because she was embarrassed by what had happened between them but more so because the reality that they had become as one seemed somehow reverent, or so Annora felt. The sky lightened into a pink and orange display that foretold that the day would be bright. Richard bent forward and once more claimed her lips before he cupped her cheeks to stare directly into her eyes.

"You and I have now been etched into one another's souls, Annora. Once we have returned Meregate to your care, we shall make our plans so that we may forever remain together," he vowed sealing his words with another kiss.

She wound her arms around his neck as he again deepened the exchange between them. Aye… they had finally claimed one another and Annora could only pray to the heavens above that no further obstacles would lay in their path to their future happiness.

CHAPTER TWENTY-NINE

THE DAYS THAT followed as they continued moving forward toward Meregate merged one into the other. Richard was accustomed to spending hours in the saddle. What he was not used to was being distracted by a tawny-haired, green-eyed vixen whose smile continued to leave him flustered. His mind should be on what the upcoming demands of the castle's siege would entail. Yet his mind continually wandered to an early morn in a river with Annora's legs wrapped around his waist whilst he made her his in every way.

He had been surprised to see her at the river's edge and remembered fondly when she began to strip her clothes from her luscious body. She had the strong, well-formed body of a Viking shield maiden but was still soft in all the right places. His mouth watered in remembrance of the moment when he had lowered her onto his more than ready manhood. Aye… she had been a perfect fit once she had become accustomed to his size.

During the past several days, Richard had only wanted her more but the occasion to be together did not come again, forcing them to stay at a distance. Her two knights seemed to hover over her more than ever, much to his dismay. Or mayhap now that he and the lady had found a common accord, he just noticed their protectiveness more than usual. But even if they had withdrawn, Richard knew that he would have struggled to find time to lie in her arms, given how busy he was kept by other concerns. He cursed the duties that had kept him so unendingly occupied.

He hoped he would convince her to stay with him in his tent once they set up camp on the outskirts of Meregate. 'Twould be her choice for he had made a promise to himself that he would in no way force her into anything anymore. If she did not wish to be with him of her own accord, Richard would simply need to learn to find a bit of patience. How he prayed that that would not be necessary, though. His longing for her was so deep that he was not sure how much more he could take.

"Something has changed in you," Blake mumbled riding next to him.

Richard slid a quick glance at his friend before returning his attention back to the road ahead of them. "I am the same as I always have been," he replied sounding more sullen than convincing. *God's wounds!* Richard swore. He was beginning to think he was becoming soft. His feelings for Annora had become clearer by the day, but he would not have those feelings be easily read from his countenance. Not when he needed the men who served under him to see him as a fierce warrior rather than a soft-hearted lover. He could not let his feelings for the lady overcome his responsibilities. If Blake could see the difference, then so could the rest of the men. 'Twould not be good to lose face with those he commanded.

Blake sniggered. "You cater to the lady as though she is your lady wife. You do not think someone who has ridden and fought besides you all these years would see the change that is happening in front of me?" Blake inquired as he shifted in his saddle.

"She is a woman and 'tis my responsibilities to see to her comfort," Richard retorted hotly as he turned a scowling glare toward the annoying knight.

Blake raised his hand as though in surrender. "You do not have to take out your frustration on me, Grancourt. I only stated I noticed something different in you. 'Tis clear to anyone with eyes that you favor her."

Richard huffed. "Aye, I suppose I do. Lady de Maris has gone through many trials in her short life. I only seek to ensure she does not tire during our journey."

Blake chuckled. "That lady has been defending herself for many a year and from what I have heard, is a very capable swordswoman. I highly doubt she will tire easily whilst marching to save her people. She can take care of herself and her own needs."

A snort of disdain left Richard. "Then what good am I to her if I cannot protect her?" he mumbled, only half aware that he was voicing his thoughts aloud.

Blake's laughter erupted. "'Tis worse than I thought. You love her!"

Richard was about to say Blake spoke a falsehood but to deny his feelings for Annora felt like a betrayal to the love they had come to realize between them. "Quiet, you dolt," Richard scolded with a menacing glare of warning. "Do you have to alert everyone within hearing that a mere girl has brought me to this state of weakness?"

"The Norwood brothers would be amused to see that you, too, have finally fallen for the charms of a beautiful woman," Blake jested with him until he grew serious. "Honestly though, Richard… she is a fine woman of noble character. You will not find a better lady to take as your wife."

A huff left him. 'Twas not that Richard disagreed with anything his friend had said, but rather that the consequences of those feelings unsettled him. "She makes me… lose awareness of what I should be doing when she is near," he confessed honestly.

"I have heard the emotion of love can be… distracting. Your secret is safe with me," Blake said with a wink.

Richard glanced again at the knight riding beside him. He had the notion Blake would ride as fast as he could to find Kingsley and tell the other man such startling news. When Richard heard Annora's bubbly laughter echoing behind him, his heart lurched in his chest just from knowing she was near. She was going to drive him mad with wanting her. In that moment, he decided he was done in his attempts to keep himself from her company.

"Keep the men moving forward but scout out an area to sleep for the night. We should reach Meregate by mid-morn if we are lucky," Richard ordered before pulling on Noble's reins and moving his steed to the side of the road to await a certain someone. His whole day brightened when he finally saw his lady riding around the bend in the road.

When she moved her horse abreast of his own, she pulled on the reins and then stretched out her arm. He easily reached over to grasp her hand, barely restraining himself from pulling her from her saddle into his lap. But such a public display might only prove to the men he had other things on his mind than an upcoming siege.

"I have not had to chance to have speech with you all day, Richard," she admitted with eyes sparkling in delight. Clearly she was pleased he had taken a moment to spend with her.

He watched her intently wondering when, and more importantly how, had he fallen so completely in love with this woman. He had never been one to believe in love at first sight but if Richard thought long and hard about the matter, he may have indeed fallen to the emotion of love when he first espied Annora fighting at Winchester. He had admired her swordsmanship both then and when he had found her again during the battle at the city of Oxford.

"Richard?" she whispered softly whilst doing her own search of what was possibly troubling him. "Is there something amiss?"

He shook himself out of his own thoughts, not wishing to allow his emotions to get the better of him.

"Nay. I only wished to ensure that you were doing well. We will be making camp for the night shortly," Richard said before he leaned over in his saddle. When she also bent toward him, he placed a kiss upon her lips. Her subtle sigh of contentment made him smile.

Laughter from the men who saw their display as they rode by caused Richard and Annora to break off their brief kiss. She appeared disappointed that they were interrupted and Richard could not agree more. They had no privacy riding with an army this size.

"We should reach Meregate on the morrow," Annora mentioned confirming what Richard had already said to Blake. "Do you think Tashe will surrender easily if he is still in charge?"

Richard scowled thinking about the little Annora had told him of the man who had killed her husband and starved her people. "I do not hold much hope that Stephen kept his word to replace the man. But you know the scoundrel better than I. What do you think?"

She seemed pleased he had asked her opinion but soon her face fell in despair. "'Twas hopeful thinking on my part that he might be gone but nay, I do not think it likely. He will do all in his power to keep Meregate from me."

"Well, we shall find out the fate of your home soon enough. Ride with me until we make camp… that is if your men can manage without your company," he teased trying to lighten their mood.

Annora giggled. "I am certain Manfred and Percival will be happy to not watch over me for a spell. They have been trying to keep me amused whilst we travel but to be honest, I have missed your company and do not like that we have not had a chance to… well…" She blushed a becoming shade of pink and he knew for certain she was remembering their coupling.

Richard reached over and placed his hand on her arm. His thumb made circular motions until he noticed her shiver. He wondered if mayhap she also felt those tiny electric currents racing up her arm whenever they touched.

"I have missed your company as well, my lady, which is why I pulled Noble over to wait for you."

"Then let us spend the rest of the ride with one another. Tell me more of your sister Beatrix and her wedding to your friend Oswin.

Was their union a love match?" she asked as they continued forward, following after the other knights.

The rest of the afternoon was pleasant as he told Annora tales of his sister, Oswin, and other antics with the Norwood brothers back when they were children. When her laughter rang out in the afternoon air, he wished he could keep such a pleasant expression on her face and keep her constantly happy and at her ease. But Meregate was only a day away and when they finally reached her home, the real ordeal would begin. He had the notion that the fight ahead of them would not be an easy one.

CHAPTER THIRTY

Meregate Castle

AN OVERWHELMING RUSH of anger raced through every inch of Annora's weary body. How she wished she could break down with her own two fists the barrier keeping her from her son. She tilted her head back staring up at the huge wooden door behind the spiked portcullis that was buried deep in the ground. 'Twould take more than her strength alone to break down such an obstacle. Aye… every knight they had brought with them would need to be involved including the weight of a heavy battering ram. She was unsure how much more her heart could take knowing her son resided just on the other side of these barriers.

A reassuring hand was placed around her shoulders and Richard bent down to whisper in her ear. "We will save him, Annora. Have no fear."

"I have been scared for my son's safety from the moment I was parted from his side. Until he is in my arms again, I will worry over his well-being," she confessed with a catch in her terrified voice.

Richard pulled her closer. "Given all you have told me of Leif, he will be fine. We just need to convince whoever holds Meregate to release it back into your control."

She wished to believe 'twould be as simple as he had said, but the heaviness of her heart betrayed her. She could not help but feel that she had failed her people and son. "I know you and I have good intentions of this fiasco being over soon, Richard, but let us face the truth of the matter. I cannot imagine the steward giving up the castle so readily—especially if it is still Tashe in that role."

The earl stepped forward as he, too, assessed the castle. "I will admit the defenses of your castle are indeed superior and will hinder our ability to easily breach them."

Richard nodded. "My hope had been that the steward would have been lacking in making repairs from when Stephen overtook the place."

"Tashe had taken little pains to make any repairs that I could see when I was last here. But much to my dismay, this is no longer the case. The repairs leave me to believe that another is now controlling Meregate," Annora declared sourly. They looked upwards again to see if the steward would finally grace them with his company on the battlement walls above. For a certainty, his guards had informed them of their presence by now. It only remained to be seen how he would respond. 'Twas highly doubtful he would open the portcullis to have a conversation with them without the security of the barred entrance.

The small group standing before the castle entrance moved backward when the sound of the chainmail from the knights above proved they were making a stand on the battlement high overhead. A dozen knights that Annora did not recognized formed a line giving further proof that her own men were most likely rotting away once more in the bowels of Meregate's dungeon.

Annora shielded her eyes from the sun as she searched for sight of at least one familiar face. She grimaced when her worst fears were confirmed. Merek had been unable to take back the castle in her name. A scuffle above their heads broke out and her hand went to her throat when Clifton Tashe stepped forward with her son's tunic clenched in one meaty fist. The boy cried out her name.

"Is that Tashe?" Richard asking, taking a hold of her hand and giving it a squeeze. He then exchanged a silent look with Earl Robert.

"Aye," she murmured. Anger like she had never felt before consumed her knowing Stephen had not kept his word to replace the man who thought more of himself than those he would govern. Richard was right... Stephen would have sooner seen her die on some battlefield than to ever let her govern Meregate again.

"Leif," Annora whispered but before she could call the cur out for his rough treatment of a mere boy, the earl stepped forward and took over the situation.

"Clifton Tashe, you are hereby ordered to surrender Meregate Castle in the name of Empress Matilda," Robert bellowed whilst keeping his hand upon the hilt of his sword.

Laughter erupted from Tashe as he gave Leif a shake. "I do not answer to some lackey for a woman whose attempt to gain England's throne has failed her. My allegiance is to King Stephen, so begone with you."

"Lackey?" Richard snarled softly at the insult to the earl. "I wish this scum was before me so I could gut him like a pig."

The earl chuckled. "You may yet have your chance, Richard." Robert seemingly let the insult slide before he took one look upon Annora. "Lady de Maris, mayhap 'twould be best if you removed yourself from this confrontation."

Annora shook her head, lifting her chin. "Nay. I will remain, my lord." A snort left the earl as if he waited for her to collapse. But Annora was made of sterner stuff, and despite her fear for her son, she would not give Tashe the satisfaction of witnessing her fainting.

"Very well," the earl replied before once again giving his attention to the commotion taking place on the battlements. "At the very least, release Leif de Maris and so that we may return him to his mother."

"The boy goes nowhere. He is the reason the lady has fought for the King. I can see for myself that once you leave my gates, I will need to inform His Majesty that her allegiance has changed."

"They are not *your* gates, you bloody cur," Annora shouted, foolishly letting Tashe's words get under her skin.

"Tsk, tsk, Annora… is that any way to have speech with the man who watches over your son?" he questioned her before shoving Leif to one of his knights. "Take him back to his room and be sure there is a guard at his door."

"Leif, we *will* save you," Annora yelled at the frightened boy before he was taken from her view.

Tashe leaned an arm on the stone wall to look down upon them. "Begone with you," Clifton repeated, but the sly grin on his face was a warning to those standing below that he had a sinister trick in mind.

They jumped back quickly—and just in time before a large vat of scalding oil was emptied. Richard took her arm as they ran a short distance away. Tashe's men laughed at their plight. They had at least made an attempt to get the man to see reason, but Annora had already known Tashe was a stubborn lout. He would never willingly give in to their demands.

The earl began to storm away with Richard and Annora following him. "Set up camp, Grancourt. We will be here for a while," the earl said as he went to see to his own lodgings.

Once they were alone, Richard pulled Annora into his arms and she rested her head upon his chest. "I want my son," she cried before her sobs were muffled as she buried her face in his tabard.

"You will have him soon, my dearest," Richard replied as he smoothed down her hair. He took her chin so he could stare into her eyes. "We must needs make camp. Will you stay with me or should I have another tent set up for you?"

"You have to ask?" she queried with a confused frown.

"I do not wish to take anything from you that you would not willing give, Annora. Never again will I take you hostage or hold you against your will. The first two times nearly did me in since it went against all I hold dear."

She reached up to caress his cheek. "I do not wish to be parted from you, Richard. Aye… I will stay with you for always."

"Your words give me hope for our future," Richard stated leaning down to place a quick kiss upon her lips. "Let us away and see to getting ourselves settled. The sooner we can claim Meregate, the soon our lives together as a family can begin."

She took his arm as he escorted her back toward her horse and the rest of the men. She only looked over her shoulder once to gaze upon her home. She vowed she would free her son and people soon even if 'twas the last thing she ever did. Let the siege of Meregate begin!

CHAPTER THIRTY-ONE

Meregate Castle
One Fortnight Later

RICHARD WAS AT his wits end. For the past fortnight, Earl Robert's knights had laid siege to Annora's home. Supplies had been cut off and Richard could only ponder how many provisions Meregate's people still had left. Surely their food was running low by now. He worried that if this did not come to an end soon, the castle's inhabitants and his lady's son would all starve to death. And still, those inside showed no signs of surrendering. He and the earl needed to come up with a different plan since their efforts thus far had not worked.

Annora had become increasingly despondent. 'Twas hardly a surprise, considering her son was still being held captive. Richard could not blame her for worrying over her child, but this only made Richard feel useless when it came to offering any sort of aid. What else could they do? Perchance 'twas time to have a traction trebuchet built so that they could propel projectiles to wreck the most damage. 'Twas a common enough siege weapon, but Annora's reluctance held Richard back, given that she had said—quite truthfully—that 'twould take years to repair the damage. He had no wish to destroy the home she loved so dearly, and yet Richard was beginning to run out of other options to advance their goals.

Kingsley stood at the opening to his tent. He stood there with a grin plastered on his face that was deeply annoying. After all, these were not happy times and their situation was nothing to smile like a jackal over. "I have a surprise for you," he said chuckling.

Richard looked up from the plans of the castle with a raised brow. "I do not know what you think might be so amusing, but I am in no mood for whatever jest you might make on my behalf."

"Step outside for but a moment," Kingsley urged holding back the flap of his tent. "'Pon my honor, 'twill be worth the effort on your part and may offer you a much-needed reprieve of wracking your brain over how to gain access to Meregate."

"Very well," he mumbled thinking the fresh air might do him good. If nothing else, it might clear his head. He had just stepped out of his tent when a sight met his eyes that caused him to rock back on his heels. 'Twas the last thing he had ever expected to see.

"I think our job is done, brothers. We have left Richard Grancourt speechless," Wymar Norwood declared from atop his brown steed Aris.

"There is a first time for everything, it appears," Theobald Norwood laughed whole heartedly.

Reynard Norwood jumped down from his own horse and came up to Richard first. "Hopefully we are not too late to join in on the battle for the Empress."

Richard clasped the younger man's arm. "You are most welcome."

Wymar dismounted as did Theobald and all four men formed a circle around one another in a show of the deep and abiding friendship that had begun when they were young children. "You have been missed, Richard," Wymar said quietly before they clasped one another at their shoulders. They bent their heads forward in a silent gesture of camaraderie. Their childhood friendship had grown and strengthened into a deep brotherly bond, forged on bloody battlefields as they fought beside each other, shoulder to shoulder. Richard was touched at the emotions that filled him as he was once more amongst these fearless men.

"What the bloody hell are you all doing here? Do you not have your own lands and wives to see to?" Richard asked as he finally found his voice.

"Earl Robert sent a runner with a missive to join you here," Theobald answered whilst looking between his two brothers. "Reynard joined me along the way, and we stopped at Brockenhurst for Wymar."

Wymar nodded. "We brought what men we could spare as you can probably see from the mayhem that is adding to your camp. Our wives, on the other hand, were none too pleased that we were called back into action for our Empress."

Reynard nodded. "Aye. My own Elysande complained until I reminded her that we were still at the beck and call of Empress Matilda whenever she might have need of the strength of our swords."

Richard could only stare at the men before him. He shook his head in wonderment that they were really there. He looked at the youngest Norwood brother. "How goes your own repairs to Blackmore?"

"Slow but we are managing." Reynard looked toward Meregate and waved a gloved hand at the gate. "I thought by now the door would have at least been breached."

Richard ran his hand through his hair. "There is a problem," he began before Wymar chuckled.

"There always is," Wymar said knowingly. "And just what has caused your delay in taking this castle?"

"Lady Annora de Maris…" Richard answered whilst his eyes searched the field of people for her.

Theobald slapped Richard's back. "A pretty woman has caught your eye! 'Tis long overdue. So, are you trying to rescue her from within?"

"'Tis a bit more complicated than rescuing a lady. Besides, much like your own ladies, Ceridwen and Ingrid, Annora can rescue herself." Richard folded his arms over his chest and gave the men a smug grin.

Reynard laughed. "I am most thankful that my own lady has neither the need nor the desire to lift a sword to help protect our home."

Wymar reached over to take hold of Richard's forearm again. "Let us have speech, just you and I. Theobald and Reynard can see to our horses and get our men settled."

Richard's gaze went to Kingsley. "Find Lady Annora and ask her to join us when she has a moment," he said with a nod.

Kingsley shrugged. "That request might take some time. I think our forces just doubled."

Richard watched the other men leave to go about their business while Wymar followed him into his tent. He went to a small table and poured them each a goblet of wine. They raised their cups in a silent toast to one another and took a drink. When the two men were seated, Wymar set his goblet back down on the table. He leaned forward resting his forearms on his legs.

"You should have sent a missive yourself," Wymar said in a scolding tone, as if Richard was a young cadet under his command who he thought should have had more sense.

Richard lifted one dark brow and then shrugged. "The three of you were enjoying wedded bliss. I saw no reason to send for you when you had your hands full with your own problems and lands."

A low growl came from Wymar. "There is no problem that we have not been able to solve when we put our heads together. Now is no different simply because the Norwood brothers are now married."

Richard swiped at the back of his neck. "It makes every bit of difference, and you know this is true. I was not about to be the one to possibly have to send a missive to your wives to tell them that you had died in battle on my behalf and would not make it home. I would have never forgiven myself."

"Then 'tis a good thing the earl thought of asking us for himself. *God's wounds*, Richard! You should have sent word the moment you left for Meregate," Wymar complained bitterly.

"I did not wish to risk your life when this burden was my own to bear," Richard replied honestly, "but I *am* glad to see you."

A smirk of satisfaction lit his friend's visage. "I should hope so. Now, tell me of your lady, for I have the notion you have found your mate."

Richard began to weave his story from when he first encountered the lovely Annora on the battlefield of Winchester. The battle seemed like ages ago and for the next hour, he told his dearest friend all he had endured both on the Empress's behalf and that of his lady. He continued to watch the entrance of his tent for signs of Annora and could only ponder what was taking Kingsley so long to find her. God help him if she had gotten herself into any trouble.

CHAPTER THIRTY-TWO

Annora stood with Manfred and Percival as she paced the area. She finally halted her progress and lifted her chin as she contemplated the rounded tower. 'Twas a slim possibility for someone to scale the uneven stones, but she believed that it could be done if such a person was sure footed enough and had no fear of heights. She only needed to find someone with enough courage to undertake the task.

As much as she wished she could perform the deed herself, she was not foolish enough to believe that Richard would ever allow her to risk her life in such a manner. He had been overly protective of late, even though the sword at her side continued to prove she could take care of herself. Still, she would not try his patience by insisting on taking such a risk. He just worried for her and rightly so. Such was your fate when you found yourself in love, she supposed.

"'Tis a mad plan, Lady Annora," Manfred declared interrupting her thoughts.

"Aye," Percival interjected. "Who would be foolish enough to make such an attempt? Why, they could get halfway up, miss their footing, and easily fall to their death."

A heavy sigh left her. "There has to be a way to gain entrance to the castle. This may be the only one. We will have to ask for someone to volunteer."

Percival had a snort of disdain leave his lips. "No one would be stupid enough to volunteer for such a task, my lady. Even if you offered enough coins to line their coffers for the rest of their life, 'twould never be enough to risk falling to their peril."

Annora threw up her hands. "Well, someone has to be brave enough to give it a try," she cried out in frustration.

Manfred shook his head. "I do not think you could ply such a person with enough drink for them to agree to such an endeavor."

Annora contemplated the tower again as she mentally scaled the wall of uneven stones. "I know I could do it. I would only need to reach the second story window. Once inside, I know the layout of the castle and could easily find my way to opening the portcullis thus allowing our men entrance to take the castle."

Percival scowled. "I may not know Richard Grancourt well, but I know enough of him to be certain that he would never allow the woman he plans to take to wife to risk her life on such a doomed endeavor."

She bit her lower lip in uncertainty, thinking through how it might play out. Even once she was inside, there would still be risks aplenty. She would need help to turn the huge wheels to lift the gate which meant she would need to free her men who she was certain resided once more in the dungeon. With their aid…it could be done. It *all* could be done, and the castle could be taken at last. But how would she convince Richard this was their only choice in order to see her son and people set free? When the two men began arguing between them, she knew she would have to work hard at the task when she had speech with Richard.

She at last came out of her musings. "Richard will see reason with this plan," Annora declared hoping rather than believing that her words were the truth.

"Ha! You best learn more about your future husband, my lady, if you think he would allow you to scale such an obstacle," Manfred scoffed crossing his arms over his chest.

"Aye," Percival agreed mimicking Manfred's stance. "He will never permit it, my lady. Even if he did give his consent, I would rather undertake the task myself before allowing you to put one foot in your own attempt… and I do not care for heights."

"I appreciate your offer to go in my place, Percival, but I have to try," she said struggling to sound as though this task would not be all that difficult to achieve.

Manfred shook his head. "You can try all you wish, Lady Annora, but you will fail."

Annora was about to make a sharp retort when Kingsley came rushing to their group.

"There you are, Lady Annora. I have been looking everywhere for you," he said out of breath.

"As you can see you have found me, Sir Goodee," Annora answered tearing her eyes from contemplating the tower.

"What are you doing this close to the perimeters of Meregate? Do you not know you could easily be pierced by an arrow at this range?" Kingsley inquired with a frown.

She pushed back a lock of her hair that had become loose from her braid. She had not thought of arrows raining down upon them but the fact that she saw no movement along the battlement wall implied that there was little to fear, and that no archers had been put into place there. An oversight of Tashe's that she would like to put to her own advantage.

"What is happening that you have need of me? Has something occurred at the front gates?" she asked hopeful that this might be over soon, and that Tashe had finally come to realize that they could not survive much longer under the current state of siege.

"Nay, nothing of such import. Richard has sent me to find you," Kingsley replied offering her his arm. "I swear I'm reduced to an errand boy.

"I am certain you will be able to raise your sword soon in the name of the Empress so lead on, Sir Goodee," she said with a wave toward the direction he had come from. She had no need for his assistance and was perfectly capable of managing the distance to Richard's tent, but the knight seemed to take it as a point of honor to lead her there himself, and she saw no reason to quarrel with him.

When they drew close, Annora was surprised to hear raucous laughter coming from within. The murmur of male voices proclaimed there were several men inside and she hesitated to step inside her dwelling.

"Who is—"

"The Norwood brothers have arrived, upon summons from the earl, to give us aid, my lady. Richard asked that you join them," Kingsley answered before holding back the flap of the tent for her to enter.

The Norwood brothers! She gulped, thinking of their reputations, famed throughout the land. The elder brother—Wymar, if she recalled correctly—was called the Knight of Darkness for a reason. She had heard of his skill at the battle of Lincoln. Theobald, the middle one, was hailed as the Knight of Chaos, and he, too, had been known to have saved the Empress when Winchester fell, and they fled. Even the youngest named Reynard was reputed to be called the Knight of Havoc. She had seen him briefly when she was captured at Oxford on that cold winter night. Richard had teased her one eve that even he had learned he was reputed to be called the Knight of Mayhem. Their skill with their blades and fighting techniques were the stuff that legends were made of.

"Lady Annora?" Kingsley murmuring her name pulled her out of her thoughts of the men she was about to encounter.

"Aye... of course," she finally answered as she stepped forward into the tent and Kingsley fell in behind her.

Five men lounged inside at a table—Richard, Blake, and three men with whom she was largely unfamiliar. With cups in hand, they appeared as though this was no more than a social gathering of friends despite the siege taking place outside. Kingsley went to the table, poured himself a chalice of wine, and took a vacant seat.

The knight with dark wavy hair and green eyes slammed his tankard on the table. "This is her?" he bellowed cheerfully. "I can see why you are so smitten, Richard."

Another man with shorter light-brown hair and blue-green eyes reached over to slap his brother's arm. "Be respectful, you dolt," he declared with a frown before rising to his feet to bow to her. "Forgive my brother's lose tongue, my lady."

Him coming to a stand seemed to pull the rest of the gentleman from their stupor as they, too, rose to their feet.

Richard crossed the short distance and took hold of her hand, pulling her forward. "Lady Annora de Maris, may I present to you my friends," he began pointing to each man as he introduced them, "Wymar, Theobald, and Reynard Norwood."

The one called Reynard chuckled. "Friends? I would think we are more like brothers than mere friends."

Richard tossed the younger man a smirk. "I stand corrected. 'Tis been some time since we were all together in one room."

"Gentlemen," Annora said with a nod of her head. "Your aid in this cause is most welcome."

Wymar came forward and bowed before her. "We would do anything in our power to aid Richard... and our Empress."

Theobald reached out for a pitcher and poured wine into another goblet. He stood before her and offered her the cup. "We are most pleased to finally meet the woman who has captured our brother's heart. We were unsure if this day would ever come," he said merrily. He lifted his cup high. "To the Lady Annora!"

Annora raised her cup at his toast before taking a sip. To be so readily accepted among them should bring her a fair amount of pleasure but the dire situation of Meregate continued to weigh on her mind. Richard ushered her to a chair and when she took a seat, she set her goblet down on the table.

"Where have you been?" Richard asked raising her hand to his lips. "I was worried when it took Kingsley so long to find you."

Annora's gaze touched on each of the knights at the table before she returned her attention to Richard. Now was as good of a time as any to tell him of her idea.

"I was at far side of Meregate inspecting one of the towers," Annora began. She hadn't even touched upon her plan as yet, and already a scowl of worry etched its way across Richard's brow.

"Are you mad to risk your life by getting so close?" he asked.

"Did I say I was close? For all you know I was a respectable distance away," she huffed in annoyance even as she secretly admitted that his words rang true. She had become so lost in her plan that she had not even considered arrows from above that might harm her.

A snort left Richard. "After these many months together, you do not think I know of your reckless nature where Meregate and your son are concerned? Of course, you were too close," Richard replied reaching for his cup and downing the contents.

The men broke out into laughter although Annora did not feel this was anything to jest over.

Wymar leaned his elbow on the table. "You have your hands full with this one, Richard," he beamed with a roguish grin. "The lady will fit in well with our wives since they are all of a similar nature."

Reynard banged his tankard on the table. "A lady who can hold her own against the Knight of Mayhem! He is blessed." The other men began imitating the youngest Norwood knight and Annora could see for the bond between this group did indeed go beyond mere friendship.

Richard held up his hand and the men finally settled down. "I assume you came up with some plan that might bring down Tashe."

"I have, although you may not like what you hear." Annora heard the grunt of disapproval before she even uttered anything further. "Please hear me out, Richard, before you decide whether or not 'twill work. I believe 'tis a sound plan, for all that it has its risks."

Theobald took another long pull of his drink. "Aye… she will fit in perfectly with our wives."

Richard shot Theobald a warning glare. "Very well, Annora. I will make every attempt to remain open minded."

"This should prove interesting," Wymar said chuckling.

Another round of jesting at Richard's behalf began again with Blake and Kingsley joining in on the group's merriment. She drummed her fingers upon the wooden table before they at last quieted down enough to listen to her words.

"Since our waiting game has gotten us nowhere near to having Meregate freed from Tashe's grasp, I propose we arrange an attack at the front gate. With enough force of a battering ram, the portcullis will eventually crack along with the door barring our way into the inner bailey. The most important part is that those at the front will keep Tashe's men preoccupied," she began, though she could not keep the worry from her brow as she contemplated where her real plan would take place.

Richard's own brow arched upward. He did indeed know her well. "And…?"

Reynard leaned forward. "You think there is more to her plan?"

Richard nodded. "Anything and everything is possible with this particular lady," he said with an appreciative grin. "Please continue, Annora."

She took a deep breath and held on to what she knew would erupt from the man she loved. "Whilst the men are busy at the front, I will scale the tower at the rear. I have been studying the layout and the stones are uneven enough that I believe I can climb up to at least the second story. I'll slip inside and make my way to turn the wheel to open the gates."

Richard's mouth opened several times before he snapped his lips shut. And then his anger got the better of him and his voice exploded inside the confinement of the tent. "Absolutely not!" he bellowed in outrage. "God's blood, woman, do you honestly think I would allow you to undertake such a task?"

"I'm light enough to scale the wall without too much difficulty, and once inside, I am the one who is best suited to take advantage of the situation, given how well I know the layout of the castle. Tashe's men will be distracted by the frontal attack, and none will see me coming. The plan makes sense," she said crossing her arms over her chest.

Richard threw up his hands. "Aye! If you wish a death sentence. We will find another way," he howled in frustration.

"There is no other way. Any longer and my son might die of starvation," she yelled back at him.

Chaos ensued between everyone gathered in Richard's tent, and voices became raised as each knight attempted to get their point across over the other. Annora sat back and listened as they tried to come up with something that might not be so risky. In the end, they all turned to Annora who began again to outline her idea to scale a tower to free her son.

CHAPTER THIRTY-THREE

*B*Y *SAINT MICHAEL'S Wings*! This had to be the most insane quest he had ever undertaken in his entire life. The day had just dawned. The steady beat of the battering ram hitting the front gates echoed in the distance. The sun was only a sliver on the horizon, giving just enough light to find the path upward he must take when Richard began his climb. Aye! *His* climb for he would in no way allow the woman who meant all to him to risk her life on something so dangerous. If one of them was to hazard a treacherous climb and the potential for a deadly fall, then 'twould not be his lady.

He reached upward to grab at another stone in order to pull himself upward. The progress was slow, and he had lost count on the number of times where he had dangled by one arm before he was able to gain the next perch. This was an asinine plan even though he had agreed with Annora that it could possibly work. But there was a problem with he reached the shutter of the second story window. Annora had told him that the clasp was loose and that 'twould be easy to push open the wood. What she did not know was that someone had repaired the clasp, leaving Richard with the options to either return down to the ground in defeat or move upward to the third story window to make another attempt and hope that the higher shutter would be less secure.

He was trying to determine the best course of action when he heard a sound from above. All their plans would be for naught if they were caught, and Richard was waiting for his fate, praying he would not die by scalding oil being poured upon him. He would rather die with his sword in his hand than by any other method. He was surprised to see a tawny-haired boy poke his head from the third floor window and lean down to call to him.

"The way is clear, Sir Knight," he said with a mischievous grin before disappearing back inside.

Richard had the notion he had just espied Annora's son who appeared to be as clever and resourceful as his mother. Having hope that all would work out, Richard began to climb again but worried as the stones became smaller, making it far more difficult to find a holding. He was in the process of wondering how he might be able to climb the rest of the way when a rope was let down. He gave it a tug. Thankfully the lifeline seemed as though it might hold his weight.

The boy came back, and this time he was with a woman. "The rope will not fail you, Sir Knight," she said reassuringly, and Richard could only offer up a prayer that this would be true. There was only one way to find out.

With a brief petition to the heavens above, he took hold of the rope and began to climb hand over hand until he reached the ledge of the window. The woman and boy took hold of his arms and pulled. They all tumbled to the stone floor in a heap. Richard let out a sigh of relief. With their help, he had made it.

The woman untangled her gown from around her legs and stood up to rush across the room to offer Richard a drink. When he had quenched his thirst, he stood to survey the bedchamber and its occupants.

"My thanks for your assistance. I do not believe I would have made it without you," Richard said gratefully.

"Thought you were going to die about halfway up," the boy said with a laugh. "But you proved yourself capable in the end."

"And you are?" Richard asked already knowing the boy's answer.

"Leif de Maris. Are you here to rescue us?" he asked with hopeful green eyes so much like his mother's Richard had no doubt as to the lad's identity.

"Aye. I am Lord Richard Grancourt. Your mother sent me."

The boys chin quivered. "Is she well?"

Richard placed his hand on the boy's shoulder, fighting to keep from frowning when he could tell by the boniness that the child had been without food for some time. "She will be once you are back in her keeping." He turned to the woman.

"My name is Edme. I was Lady de Maris's maid when she was here. I have been trying to watch over the young master," she said placing her own hand on the lad's shoulder. "We were not sure how much longer we could hold out."

"I am here now, as is Lady de Maris. Meregate will soon be back in her control," Richard said in what he hoped sounded reassuring. "Where are the men Lady de Maris set free the last time she was here along with her captain?"

"Back where she found them. In the dungeon," Leif proclaimed crinkling his nose in disgust.

Edme nodded. "I have been trying to sneak food to them to the best of my ability but with supplies running low there is not much to offer anyone."

Richard swore beneath his breath. He was not surprised by their location, but he feared there would be no chance for them lending any sort of aid if they were weakened from hunger. The most important thing now was to get the gate opened. Could he manage it alone? He started to quickly rethink their plan.

Edme seemed to have read his mind as she offered information. "Clifton Tashe has been lazy of late thinking he is safe within these walls. But with the attempt at the front gate, I heard tell he was to send men to the battlements. I do not believe any were sent to guard the inner bailey as yet. You may still have time to raise the portcullis if you hurry."

Richard pulled his sword from the scabbard strapped to his side. "Tell me where to go."

Edme quickly gave him the instructions on the best way to remain hidden while reaching his objective of the front gate. Richard nodded before he turned to the two people who had aided him. He began to realize he might need further help.

"The boy must stay here where I know he will be safe. If anything were to happen to him, I would have to answer to Lady Annora." He gazed at the lady who had also offered her assistance and wondered if he could ask her to risk her life. He had no choice. "Do you think you could make your way to the dungeon to release the knights being held captive?"

"I can help," Leif answered for Edme.

He knelt down so he was on the boy's level. "I would rather keep you safe in this chamber, young Leif."

The boy frowned and was about to respond when Edme held the boy back from bolting toward the door. "Lord Grancourt is right. You must be kept safe at any cost," she replied patting the lad on his thin shoulder. She raised her eyes to Richard once he stood. "I can do it, my lord."

"Then let us get to work to return Meregate to its rightful owner, in the name of Empress Matilda. If I run into trouble, I can only pray those kept against their will have enough strength remaining to join me in freeing Meregate. I doubt I will be able to turn the wheel to raise the portcullis on my own, although I will try," Richard proclaimed ruffling Leif's hair. "Stay here and bolt the door when we leave."

"I could help more on the other side of the door instead of being stuck here by myself," Leif complained bitterly.

Richard choked back a laugh at the stubbornness of his face. Aye, he was a replica of his mother for certain. They left the room and the sound of the bolt being slid into place gave Richard a fair amount of satisfaction that Annora's son was at least safe.

He followed behind Edme through the twists and turns of the passageways. When she came to a turret, they rushed down the curving stairs, the woman moving at remarkable speed despite her age. She clearly was more than capable of doing the task he had given her.

When they reached the ground level, Edme pointed ahead. "'Tis just through that door, my lord. Afterwards, you shall need to watch your back for I know not what you shall encounter."

"Get Annora's guards free, and then together we shall take care of the rest," Richard said quietly hoping the woman would not run into any problems.

Richard watched her scurry away and gave her several minutes before he carefully made his way to one of the back doors of the keep. Opening the wooden barrier, he stole a glance outside to ensure that way was safe for him to proceed. He made every attempt to keep hidden from the knights who stood on the battlement walls, no easy task for there was not much to hide behind when he neared the openness of the courtyard. But the constant beating of the battering ram kept those above preoccupied as they watched the display below them with much amusement. They were not clever or disciplined enough to keep themselves on guard for an attack coming from an unexpected direction.

He inspected the wheels to raise the door and knew with a certainty that he would need help, for there were two that must needs be manipulated at the same time. Such a task could not be accomplished without another helping hand. 'Twas obvious that Clifton Tashe had made a few upgrades in the barricade that now kept him safe from the earl's army on the other side.

"How the bloody hell did you get in here?" a voice rang out in the early morning air.

Richard turned raising his sword to see Tashe entering the bailey with several knights behind him. Richard raised his sword and stepped forward but was pleasantly surprised to see Annora's captain along with several other men begin to fill the yard. They quickly filed in behind Richard in a show of support. He was grateful for their backing, even though he questioned how much force they could bring to bear, given that they looked as though they had indeed been starving in the depths of the dungeon.

Richard tore his gaze from the threat in front of him to Merek Baringar behind him. "Get that barrier open now or all is lost," he ordered, and a bellow of outrage was heard from Tashe. "Try not get yourselves killed in the process."

Tashe had apparently heard enough. "Kill them! Kill them all, the traitors."

Richard and the few men who stood with them raised their swords, ready for the battle ahead of them. He could only pray that they would not fail his lady.

CHAPTER THIRTY-FOUR

ANNORA STOOD BACK with Earl Robert and the Norwood brothers as she watched the men continue to batter Meregate's portcullis and door. 'Twas the only thing that stood in the way of reaching her son and Richard. There could be no mistaking the sound of a battle taking place within the courtyard. The sound of steel sheering off steel was a sound a person did not forget. How many years had she herself been thrust in the heat of one battle after another, forced to fight for her life? Too many and now her breath hitched at what awaited them inside. More than fear for her own safety, she worried about Richard's fate.

When the portcullis began to rise, she had hope for the first time this morn. The earl began bellowing orders to get the heavy gate propped up in the event that the men inside manipulating the wheels failed to continue to gain ground, and the barrier once more came crashing down. The knights fitted a heavy piece of wood between two of the spikes as an anchor, and then the earl's men began pouring into the inner bailey. Annora rushed forward with them, her sword raised to assist with the fight.

She saw her beloved Richard fighting with one of Clifton Tashe's knights. The man himself stood at a safe distance away from the fighting. Annora was not surprised that the man was too much of a coward to dirty his hands even to defend what he claimed to think of as his. Still, he shouted insults toward Richard as if to taunt the man. Annora began fighting her way to give aid if Richard should have need of it. 'Twas not hard to catch their conversation as she drew closer.

Richard slashed his sword at this adversary who fell to the ground in a moan. He then turned toward Clifton who at last raised his own blade to defend himself.

Richard aimed the point of his sword toward Tashe. "Yield the day and call off your men. You may then live to breathe yet another day," he ordered with a deepening scowl upon his brow.

Clifton smirked, no doubt feeling superior to the man before him. "You were one of the men at my gates when you arrived with the woman who will be my wife," he stated snidely.

A snort of disdain left Richard. "As was the Earl of Gloucester if you recall."

"Bah! I care not for some titled knight who is but a bastard," Clifton retorted waving his sword in front of him. "I only care that I can kill the vermin who is trying to steal my woman and this estate from me."

"She is hardly your woman," Richard scoffed with a sneer. "Look around you and concede, Tashe. The earl's men have yours surrounded and are falling one by one. You are outnumbered. If you wish to live, yield and you may be allowed to return to your own lands to live out your life."

Annora held the knight she had been fighting at bay with the tip of her blade. He held up his hands and dropped his sword. Several of the earl's men came and took the man away and she at last saw Merek rushing toward her. Thank heavens he was still alive!

She turned her attention to Richard and watched whilst panic flashed quickly across Tashe's visage. The realization that he was losing Meregate was finally penetrating his thick skull.

A bellow of outrage left him. "Who are you but some mercenary out for fame and coins to fill your coffers. Surely you jest if you think that Lady Annora would be with you."

Annora had heard enough. "You insult Lord Richard Grancourt, you scum," she said fuming in self-righteous anger.

Richard made an attempt to hold her back. "I can handle him, my dear."

"Aye, I know you more than capable, but this is my score to settle," she said stepping forward.

Richard gave a short bow and waved his hand. "Then by all means, my lady."

"You would allow a woman to fight in your stead?" Clifton tilted his head back and laughed whilst inspecting her from head to toe. "You think you can best me? A mere woman?"

"With one hand tied behind my back if necessary," Annora jeered. "Let us be done with this so I can fulfill by oath to see you in hell for killing my husband and withholding my child from me."

"You think you are so brave, but you will not win this day," Tashe declared as he swung his blade toward her head.

With his first swing, Annora could see at once that Clifton was heavy footed. While he might be strong, he was nowhere near as deft as she, nor did he have her training or experience. Annora easily dodged the move and countered quickly. As the fight continued, metal gnashed against metal and Annora clearly had the upper hand. He began to rapidly tire from his efforts.

"I am thrilled you did not yield the day as Lord Grancourt offered. I will not be so merciful after all you have done to my family and those under my care. I will gain far more pleasure knowing you died by my sword and that I will never again have to worry about you being a troublesome neighbor at the edges of my land," Annora declared as she continued swinging her blade.

"You will be my wife," he bellowed before he lunged toward Annora who ducked beneath his arm.

As she twirled around, her sword sliced at his arm, and she watched in satisfaction as the blade dropped and blood began dripping from the wound.

But still Tashe was not about to concede defeat. He pulled a dagger from the waist of his belt and began slashing the blade in front of Annora who was unbothered by this attempt as if a fly was buzzing in front of her face to pester her. Her amusement rang out only causing fury to erupt from Clifton once more.

"You bitch! I will kill you for your insolence," he screamed swinging wildly through the air with his dagger.

"Never again will you step foot on my grounds and torment me or my people," she warned with a grin, filled with satisfaction at the knowledge that she would finally have her retribution. "You took my husband's life and held my son hostage. Never again shall you harm those in my care. You shall rot in my pit after I am done with you."

Tashe swung the knife again, but he truly was no match for her skill with her weapon. Annora easily knocked the dagger from his hand and the blade went skidding across the stones of the courtyard. She was about to claim her win when she heard a voice call out "Mama!"

Distracted, she turned toward the sound, and Clifton took advantage of the moment to charge toward her, seizing hold of her sword and wrenching it from her fist.

"I hope you enjoy hell, Annora," Clifton sneered as he drew the sword above his head.

From the corner of her eye, she saw Leif toss a dagger in her direction. It fell just short of her hand. She hurriedly spun over the ground, reaching for the blade. Coming to her knees, she plunged the dagger forward and upward into the stomach of Tashe whose eyes mirrored his shock that she had succeeded in striking a fatal blow.

Her sword fell behind him with a clang before Tashe tumbled backwards. Blood splattered from his mouth as he pulled out the dagger. He grasped at the place the blade pierced his body, as if he still could not bring himself to believe that he'd been wounded.

"I will see you in hell for this," he sneered before a gurgle left him.

Then his eyes went blank and Tashe knew no more.

Annora scanned the courtyard, and she opened her arms whilst her son came running to her. She pulled the frail boy into her embrace and promised herself she would see to the feast herself to ensure he would no longer be hungry.

"You gave me such a fright," she whispered to Leif whilst he continued to keep his arms around her waist.

Richard joined them and ruffled his hair. "He is much like you, Annora. Never listens and does not stay where he is told."

Leif peeked up from the security of her arms to stare upon the knight. "I told you I could help."

"And help you did but I am certain your mother could have handled the situation herself," Richard proclaimed before reaching out to cup her cheeks. "Did he hurt you?"

"Nary a scratch." She beamed with pride. "My thanks for allowing me to dispatch the scoundrel."

"You are well rid of him. At the very least, you will not have to worry over another attack from your neighbor," Richard declared pulling Annora into his embrace.

Annora rested her head upon his chest hearing the beating of his heart. "You survived the climb," she murmured, even though that much was obvious, since she was standing here in his arms.

"I almost did not. If your son and Edme had not come to my aid, I am certain we would not now be having this conversation," Richard admitted.

Her gaze traveled to the Norwood brothers who stood with Earl Robert as they clasped each other's hands in friendship. "Do you suppose you will need to continue your service to the earl and Empress?" she asked not daring to think of being separated from Richard again.

"I will ask to be released so we might wed. That is, if you will have me," he teased bending down to kiss the top of her head.

"Gladly," she answered with a sincere heart. "Will we live here or at Lyndhurst?"

"Mayhap we shall divide our time between both, but we shall figure out our living arrangements once we have put Meregate back into proper order," Richard declared. "Come, let us go see to your people and ensure they have a proper meal. I will not have our boy starving another day."

"Our boy... I like the sound of that," Annora said smiling as she took Richard's hand and reached for Leif's.

Her future appeared secure with Richard, and as the day progressed into the eve, she could only marvel on all she had gone through to finally have all she desired. Her son safe and secure in her arms. Her home back under her control in the name of Empress Matilda. And Richard... a man she would have only dreamed of and one she would love until the end of her days. Together they would carve out a bright new future. She had found her home in the arms of the Knight of Mayhem. May their days and nights be forever peaceful.

CHAPTER THIRTY-FIVE

Meregate
One Fortnight Later

RICHARD OBSERVED THE festivities of his wedding celebration from his place at the raised dais in Meregate's great hall. His wife was dancing to a lively tune with her captain of her guard. Merek and the other knights who had been held captive had all been restored to their rightful places as part of the garrison to guard these very walls. Luckily, none had been too severely injured during their unfortunate stay in the depths of Meregate's underbelly.

The missive sent by the Earl of Gloucester had at last reached King Stephen regarding his men who had been captured at Wilton. The King had been forced to spend a small fortune to ensure those who had shielded his retreat regained their freedom. But that was not the only loss the King had been required to agree to. Any further claim to Meregate Caste was relinquished but Annora's home was not the only place that Stephen was required to forfeit. Sherborne Castle was also surrendered as payment. Such a loss stripped two more pieces of land that reinforced his control over England. The cost for having his lieutenants and men returned to him had been high.

Earl Robert had released Richard from his service but reserved the right to call upon him if the Empress found herself in need of his aid in the future. With the earl's leaving, the Norwood brothers also departed to make their journey back to their homes and the wives who awaited their return. Richard would miss their company but had promised that he and Annora would visit as soon as they could possibly travel. He still had the need to introduce his wife to his parents at Lyndhurst.

During the past fortnight, the people of Meregate regained their strength as supplies once more flowed into the castle. Annora took charge of seeing her home restored to its former glory and day by day, Meregate was slowly becoming the place his wife remembered. Her son was never far from her side and she welcomed Leif's presence. Richard could hardly blame her for wishing her child to be close. She had been parted from his company for longer than she had thought would be possible.

There had only been one moment nigh unto two se'nnight ago that had caused Richard's entire world to shift unexpectedly. He had returned to their bedchamber early one morn to find Annora still abed. Concerned for her health, he rushed to her side only for her to hold out her hand to halt his progress whilst she leaned over the bedside and lost the contents of her stomach. Bringing her something to drink, he swore she appeared positively green. When he had asked her what ailed her, her response had almost caused him to pass out cold.

"My darling Richard... There is no easy way to tell you this, but unless you want your child to be born without your name, you best call the priest soon so he might bless your union."

A child... Aye. He may have been momentarily shocked and unable to respond to her words but he had quickly recovered and from that point, he could barely contain his joy that she carried their babe within her. Richard had wasted little time in making all the arrangements and had been more than elated when he at last was able to call Annora his wife.

A gentle caress ran across his shoulders and he tilted his head back to stare into the mesmerizing green eyes of his lady.

"You were lost in thought, my love," she purred sweetly. "Good thoughts, I hope."

"Of course. They were of you," he replied pulling her down into his lap and nuzzling her neck.

"Richard, our guests! What will they think?" she laughed leaning over to kiss his cheek.

"They will think I must surely be out of my head to still be sitting here in the great hall making merry instead of taking my wife up to our chamber to have my wicked way with her," he teased in a tone that should have warned her he was about done with delaying their official union as man and wife.

Her laughter was infectious and Richard smiled with satisfaction, knowing he was the cause of her happiness.

She stole a glance around her hall before a blush rushed becomingly across her face. "You do not think they will miss us?" she inquired softly running her fingers up the front of his tunic.

"Nay, and I cannot think of a better time than now for us to head to our bedchamber," Richard said sliding his hand up her leg under the table.

She playfully swatted his hands away. "Not here, Richard. Leif is watching," she scolded with a smile that told him she was not all that put out that he wanted her.

He pulled her forward so he could whisper in her ear. "Then let us take this to our room where I can make you cry out in pleasure," he said huskily. He held out his hand for her to take and when she rose to her feet he also stood. He called for another barrel of wine to be brought up from the cellars. Meregate's people could continue on with their celebration without their lord and mistress.

Annora gave her son a hug goodnight as they made their way toward the turret and when they arrived at their room, Richard put the bolt into place to ensure their privacy for the eve. Annora went to a table by the window and poured a chalice of wine. A small repast was laid out for them to enjoy, not that Richard was hungry for any more food.

His eyes all but devoured his wife as she sipped from the cup. She held it out and he came to her. He deliberately placed his lips where hers just touched in a lover's gesture, and she beamed her approval before she began slipping out of her gown. Placing the chalice down, his hands skimmed over the lush body before him.

She wound her arms around his neck and pressed herself into his chest. "Now... what were you saying about having your wicked way with me, my lord?" she said seductively whilst running her fingers through his hair. She wiggled her body against him and a part of him rose to the occasion.

A short chuckle escaped. "I believe, my lady, 'tis time I take us on another adventure."

"I look forward to the journey, Richard."

"We shall share a lifetime's worth and more, my dearest Annora."

"Have I told you today that I love you?' she asked helping pull his tunic over his head.

"I shall never tire of hearing such a sentiment from you. I love you as well, my dearest. Yesterday, today, and for all of eternity," he vowed before sealing his words with a kiss.

He heard a moan of delight to which he responded by lifting his wife into his arms and carrying her to their bed. There was no need for further words to proclaim their love. Instead, they showed one another through the remainder of the eve the true commitment they had made to one another when they spoke their vows and the priest had sealed them together.

Aye, Richard would indeed look forward to such an adventure as spending eternity with the love of his life. 'Twas a miracle they had found one another through the mayhem of war that was now behind them. Their future together looked bright and Richard would do all in his power to see that Annora never worried about anything ever again. Her happiness was the main goal now in life and that would be more than enough to keep him satisfied.

EPILOGUE

Brockenhurst, England
Summer, 1153

R ICHARD STRETCHED OUT his legs whilst sitting on a blanket staring at the scene before him. If someone had asked him ten years ago what he would be doing this day, he most likely would have said that he would likely still be fighting for Empress Matilda's cause to gain the throne. Times had certainly changed, and he could not help but smile at the contrast as he glanced at the Norwood brothers, their wives, his sister Beatrix and her husband, and all their children playing by the distant lake. Instead of Richard and his brothers in arms raising their blades, two young lads sparred with one another with small wooden swords. Their laughter rang out in childish delight as they made an attempt to save Wymar's youngest daughter Violet from a pretend dragon.

Rolf pushed his younger cousin Dristan to the ground whilst Violet shrieked before jumping out of the way.

"I won," Rolf declared raising his wooden sword in victory.

His moment of triumph was short lived when Dristan swept his legs out from under him. Rolf tumbled to the ground and Dristan leapt on top of him. "Yield the day, cousin," Dristan laughed before Rolf joined in.

"I did not see that coming," Rolf proclaimed whilst Dristan offered his hand to help him rise.

"Which is why one day you shall follow me as I become the

champion knight for King Henry," Dristan boasted as he folded his arms across his chest. His black hair blew in the breeze whilst the red cloak he wore billowed behind him.

"I cannot follow you, you dolt," Rolf interjected. "People will know we are cousins and will think I get special treatment because I am kin."

Dristan raised his hand to his chin as he contemplated his cousin's words. "Then we shall pretend we met at a tourney. 'Twill be our own private jest, just the two of us."

Rolf laughed. "That would be funny. You must have a name to lend fear into our enemies. What will you call yourself?"

"Ha! I already have a title picked out. I shall be called the Devil's Dragon of Blackmore," Dristan answered before the children ran toward the lake's edge to splash in the cool water.

Richard turned his attention to Reynard and Theobald. "They seem to have their lives all planned out, do they not? So ambitious at such a tender age. Would that I had been so determined when I was young," Richard said chuckling at the children's antics.

Reynard raised a glass to his lips. "I believe Dristan thinks he must needs prove himself to his older cousins and his older sister Serena."

Theobald gave a snort. "I remember another young lad just as determined in his youth."

Wymar joined in with a laugh. "Always trying to prove his worth as though he feared he could not live up to the Norwood name. In the end, I believe we have all come out the better." He swept his hand before them as their wives walked and played with their children. "Our name will live on with those before us. I am most content with Wren and Violet for daughters."

Richard nodded before he smirked. "Are you hoping for a boy this time?"

Wymar's brow rose. "Boy or girl, it does not matter—but 'twould be just like Ceridwen to give me another girl to worry over. She did say she would do so after we had wed and she has thus far lived up to her words."

Theobald chuckled then took a long pull of his drink. "Aye, we are indeed blessed with our children and the women who came to love us. I for one am more than content with Rolf and Coira. I do not need to have further offspring than those two. They keep Ingrid and me busy as it is."

Richard watched Annora as she began making her way back toward him. He excused himself from the others to meet his wife halfway. He placed his hand on her protruding belly.

"Does the babe pain you, my love?" he asked after he kissed her lips.

"He or she is active today. Here... feel this."

Richard's eyes widened when he felt the heel of a tiny foot pushing from the inside of Annora's womb. "My guess is your time will be upon us before we know it."

"Aye. I would not be surprised if Ceridwen and I give birth close together." She turned her attention to her boys, one practically a grown man. "Do you think the twins will mind if the babe is a girl?"

"Ryder and Robert will learn to love the child if it is a girl and you know it. Leif, on the other hand, has already declared he plans to be overly protective of a sister," Richard said with a smile.

Annora placed her head on his shoulder as they began to return back to the adults lounging on blankets and enjoying the day. "We have been very blessed, Richard. I could not ask for a better life than the one I have found at your side."

He halted their progress and reached down to caress her cheek. "There is no other woman I would rather spend my life with than you, Annora. After all, I did fall in love with you first," he teased and took delight when he heard her laughter.

"So, we are going to have that argument again, are we?"

He held up his hands as a truce. "Well... mayhap we fell in love at the same time. You were just too stubborn to admit it at the time, if I recall correctly."

She pointed a finger at him. "You are lucky that I am so heavy with child that I cannot take you to task with my sword, my dear."

Richard pulled her into his embrace. "Soon enough you will be sparring with me and Leif again to your hearts content. In the meantime, your job is to continue carrying my child. The rest must needs wait until later."

"I will remember your words calling me stubborn," she answered but had a hard time keeping the grin from her lips.

"I am counting on it, my love."

Annora pulled on his tunic until he leaned down to kiss her lips. "I adore you… just in case I have not told you lately."

He ran his fingers through her hair and kissed her forehead. "You are the light in my life, Annora. I am forever grateful to have you to love."

As they returned to the group of adults, Richard once again took in the scene before him. Luckily, the friendship of the men he had fought beside for many a year had endured and thankfully they had all survived the darkness of war. Their lives during those times had been filled with chaos and even a bit of havoc as they maneuvered through each challenge that had come their way. But Richard was indeed thankful that they could now live out their lives in peace with their wives, children, and family at their side.

Aye, his time serving the Empress Matilda's cause was at an end. He would let their children take up their duties for the Empress's son Henry, who now ruled England. Richard had a glorious life of leisure to look forward to with Annora and their children. He was more than content with the life he now chose and the woman who held his heart.

Who would have known when he had glimpsed Annora on the battlefield at Winchester that he would one day recognize her as the other half of himself that had been missing. There was no further need for him to search for adventure or glory beyond his home. As far as he was concerned, his days of going to war were over.

He stole another glance at the men who had shaped each other's past and the women who had changed their futures. Aye... The Knights of Darkness, Chaos, Havoc and Mayhem were no more...

THE END

Sherry Ewing needs your help!

Book reviews help readers to find books, and authors to find readers. Please consider writing a review for **Knight of Mayhem**, even a few sentences telling people what you liked about the story is helpful. Reviews can be posted on BookBub, Goodreads, and on Amazon. Thank you for purchasing and reading a copy of **Knight of Mayhem**. I hope you enjoyed Richard and Annora's journey to finding love.

For links to this book and more, see Sherry's website at www.sherryewing.com

AUTHOR'S NOTE

Dearest Reader:

Thank you so much for reading a copy of ***Knight of Mayhem: The Knights of the Anarchy (Book Four)***. I hope you enjoyed Richard and Annora's journey together to finding love. After years of having this series inside my head, I'm a little sad to see it come to an end but I'm thrilled that it is finally out into the world.

Richard's story came as a pleasant surprise. Originally this series was only going to be about the Norwood brothers. But Richard became such a strong secondary character in ***Knight of Darkness***, I just knew that he needed to have his own happily-ever-after. When I began to write his story, I had a clear path on the direction it would take. Funny how my characters make it known when I've got it wrong and am starting in the wrong place.

This is why Richard's story begins when Empress Matilda makes her escape from Oxford Castle in December of 1142 although that particular scene was also depicted in ***Knight of Havoc***. It was the perfect opportunity for Richard to finally learn what drove Annora de Maris to fight for King Stephen. Matilda's escape in the middle of the night, however, put an end to the siege of Oxford once Stephen learned she was no longer inside. The surrender was indeed relatively amicable. I can only imagine his fury knowing she had again evaded caving in to his demands.

Meregate Castle is of my own making. I wanted a place for Annora's home to be somewhere near the cliffs of Dover. I wanted a location where the Empress's ships could safely dock if her husband sent reinforcements from Normandy. Margate became Meregate so I could do whatever I needed to drive my plot forward.

There was a short skirmish in Wilton in 1143 after King Stephen fled with Bishop Henry. Stephen ended up surrendering the castle of Sherborne in ransom payments for the men Earl Robert had captured who had sacrificed themselves to shield Stephen's retreat from the battlefield. I also alluded to the King having to surrender Meregate in my story. Moving my characters to Meregate was complexly fictional on my part, including any reference to the Earl of Gloucester being a part of the siege on Annora's home.

Bringing the Norwood brothers to Meregate seemed a natural conclusion to this series but even more so the epilogue. Everything came full circle, including the reason why I chose these particular years as the setting for the *Knights of the Anarchy* series. With the birth of Dristan of Blackmore (Reynard's son), I tied my MacLaren series from **If My Heart Could See You** into this one. Everything I wrote afterwards began with my debut novel including my time travels. I had another author moment writing that final scene with the young cousins. When an author sheds a tear or two at her own work, she knows she's done something right!

And one last bit of history on Empress Matilda… After Matilda fled Oxford, she went to Devizes Castle. By this time period, Matilda was beginning to come to the realization that she would never sit on England's throne and that she should look to her son Henry to become her successor. But the catalyst for this decision was the death of her half-brother Robert, Earl of Gloucester on October 31, 1147. He had been the most faithful supporter to her cause for many years—someone she could always lean on.

At that point, she accepted that she could best serve her son by distancing herself from him to clear Henry's path to the crown. In early 1148, Matilda boarded a ship for France and never returned to England again. Henry had many trials in the years that followed. When King Stephen fell ill and died in October 1154, Henry gained the throne sooner than he expected.

Once again, I relied heavily on the book *Matilda. Empress. Queen. Warrior* by Catherine Hanley for my research. But I would like to leave you with this last bit of information and a quote from that book:

> *Great by birth, greater by marriage, greatest in her offspring*
> *Here lies the daughter, wife and mother of Henry*

"Matilda was, as her epitaph stated, a daughter, wife and mother. But she was much more than that. She was a twice-crowned queen, an empress, and 'lady of the English'; she was a well-travelled, politically astute woman of the world; she was an able strategist who could understand and take advantage of complex military situations; she was someone who had a cause to believe in and who never gave up on it. In a world that expected her to be an accessory, Matilda was the master of her fate and the agent of her own destiny, and it is thus that she deserves to be remembered."

I hope I did her memory proud.

A special word of thanks to Kathryn Le Veque and the entire Dragonblade Publishing team for all their patience and hard work that comes from getting my books from my laptop into our readers' hands. It does take an entire team, and I appreciate everything you've done on my behalf.

Thank you to my amazing editor, Elizabeth Mazer. Your insight continues to amaze me on how to improve these characters. Thank you from the bottom of my heart for all you've done for me on this project. I couldn't have done this without you!

My family, especially my daughter Jessica, always has my gratitude for their patience, love, encouragement, and most of all their support when I need it the most.

A shout out to two of my readers: Carole Burant and Marianne Blair. Somewhere along the years they named the horses Shadow (Carole) and Noble (Marianne) at an event on Facebook. They get bragging rights that I used their choices. Thank you, ladies!

And last but certainly not least, a huge thank you to my incredible readers. You've been making this series an Amazon bestseller and your reviews have been lovely. I try to read them all and cannot express my gratitude enough that you've been enjoying my work. You continue to be the reason I write!

I hope you've been enjoying these author notes with insight into my series. And as I wrap up this final note up for my *Knights of the Anarchy*, I bid you all a fond farewell until the next time one of my books crosses your way. Thank you again for all your support. It means the word to me.

With much love,
Sherry Ewing

Other Books by Sherry Ewing

Medieval & Time Travel Series

Knight of Darkness: The Knights of the Anarchy (Book One)
Sometimes finding love can become our biggest weakness...

Knight of Chaos: The Knights of the Anarchy (Book Two)
In the chaos of war, can one knight defy the odds to find peace with the woman warrior he loves?

Knight of Havoc: The Knights of the Anarchy (Book Three)
One lone knight. One strongminded maiden. When duty wars with love at first sight, which will win?

Knight of Mayhem: The Knights of the Anarchy (Book Four)
Torn between duty and love, can the knight and the woman warrior forget they are enemies and let love into their hearts?

To Love A Scottish Laird: De Wolfe Pack Connected World
Sometimes you really can fall in love at first sight...

To Love An English Knight: De Wolfe Pack Connected World
Can a chance encounter lead to love?

If My Heart Could See You: The MacLarens, A Medieval Romance (Book One)
When you're enemies, does love have a fighting chance?

For All of Ever: The Knights of Berwyck, A Quest Through Time (Book One)
Sometimes to find your future, you must look to the past...

Only For You: The Knights of Berwyck, A Quest Through Time (Book Two)
Sometimes it's hard to remember that true love conquers all, only after the battle is over…

Hearts Across Time: The Knights of Berwyck (Books One & Two)
Sometimes all you need is to just believe… Hearts Across Time is a special edition box set that combines Katherine and Riorden's stories together from *For All of Ever* and *Only For You*.

A Knight To Call My Own: The MacLarens, A Medieval Romance (Book Two)
When your heart is broken, is love still worth the risk?

To Follow My Heart: The Knights of Berwyck, A Quest Through Time (Book Three)
Love is a leap. Sometimes you need to jump…

The Piper's Lady: The MacLaren's, A Medieval Romance (Book Three)
True love binds them. Deceit divides them. Will they choose love?

Love Will Find You: The Knights of Berwyck, A Quest Through Time (Book Four)
Sometimes a moment is all we have…

One Last Kiss: The Knights of Berwyck, A Quest Through Time (Book Five)
Sometimes it takes a miracle to find your heart's desire…

Promises Made At Midnight: The Knights of Berwyck, A Quest Through Time (Book Six)
Make a wish…

It Began With A Kiss: The MacLarens, A Medieval Romance (Book Four)
Sometimes you need to listen when your heart begins to sing…

Regency

A Kiss For Charity: A de Courtenay Novella (Book One)
Love heals all wounds but will their pride keep them apart?

The Earl Takes A Wife: A de Courtenay Novella (Book Two)
It began with a memory, etched in the heart.

Before I Found You: A de Courtenay Novella (Book Three)
A quest for a title. An encounter with a stranger. Will she choose love?

Nothing But Time: A Family of Worth (Book One)
They will risk everything for their forbidden love…

One Moment In Time: A Family of Worth (Book Two)
One moment in time may be enough, if it lasts forever…

A Love Beyond Time: A Family of Worth (Book Three) in the Bluestocking Belles Under the *Harvest Moon* 2023 boxset
Can love at first sight be reborn after heartbreak, proving a second chance is all you need?

Under the Mistletoe
A new suitor seeks her hand. An old flame holds her heart. Which one will she meet under the kissing bough?

A Mistletoe Kiss in the Bluestocking Belles boxset *Belles & Beaux* (2022)
All she wants for Christmas is a mistletoe kiss…

A Second Chance At Love
Can the bittersweet frost of lost love be rekindled into a burning flame?

A Countess to Remember
Sometimes love finds you when you least expect it…

To Claim A Lyon's Heart: Lyon's Den Connected World
A gambler's bet. A widow's burden. Will one game of chance change their lives?

The Lyon and His Promise: Lyon's Den Connected World
A gentleman's lifetime regret. A widow's tarnished reputation. Can they repair the past to create a bright future together?

Only A Lyon Will Do: Lyon's Den Connected World
Can a chance encounter turn desire into love?

You can find out more about Sherry's work on her website at www.SherryEwing.com and at online retailers.

Social Media for Sherry Ewing

You can learn more about Sherry Ewing at these social media links:
Amazon Author Page: amzn.to/1TrWtoy
Bookbub: bookbub.com/authors/sherry-ewing
Dragonblade Publishing:
dragonbladepublishing.com/team/sherry-ewing
Facebook: facebook.com/SherryEwingAuthor
Goodreads: goodreads.com/author/show/8382315.Sherry_Ewing
Instagram: instagram.com/sherry.ewing
Pinterest: pinterest.com/SherryLEwing
TikTok: tiktok.com/@sherryewingauthor
X: @Sherry_Ewing
YouTube: youtube.com/SherryEwingauthor
Newsletter Sign Up: bit.ly/2vGrqQM
Facebook Street Team: facebook.com/groups/799623313455472
Facebook Official Fan page: facebook.com/groups/356905935241836

About Sherry Ewing

Sherry Ewing picked up her first historical romance when she was a teenager and has been hooked ever since. An award-winning and bestselling author, she writes historical and time travel romances to awaken the soul one heart at a time. When not writing, she can be found in the San Francisco Bay Area at her day job as an Information Technology Specialist.

Learn more about Sherry where a new adventure awaits you on every page:
Website: www.SherryEwing.com
Email: Sherry@SherryEwing.com

Printed in Great Britain
by Amazon